*Selected Writings of*
*William Goyen*

# Selected Writings

## of

## William Goyen

Eight Favorites by a Master American Storyteller

Illustrated by
**ELIZABETH FAIRBANKS**

**A Random House · Bookworks book**

First printing, February 1974:  1500 copies in cloth
                                7500 copies in paperback

Cover design and illustrations by Elizabeth Fairbanks, San Francisco
Typeset by Vera Allen Composition Service, Hayward, California
      (special thanks to Rosemay and Irene)
Printed and bound under the supervision of Dean Ragland, Random
House

This book is co-published by     Random House Inc.
                                 201 East 50th Street
                                 New York, N.Y. 10022

                          and    The Bookworks
                                 1409 Fifth Street
                                 Berkeley, California 94710

Distributed in the United States by Random House, and simultaneously
published in Canada by Random House of Canada Limited, Toronto.

Library of Congress Cataloging in Publication Data

Goyen, William.
The selected writings of William Goyen.
"A Random House/Bookworks book."
I. Title.
PZ3.G748Se    813'.5'4    73-20592
ISBN 0-394-49284-6
ISBN 0-394-70691-9 (pbk.)

Manufactured in the United States of America

# TABLE OF CONTENTS

*In memory of my father,*

*Charles Provine Goyen*

# INTRODUCTION

My birthplace, once a thriving railroad and sawmill town by the Trinity River, is Trinity, located in the soft woods-and-meadows area of East Texas. My father's family brought him as a young man to Trinity from Mississippi. They were sawmill people. My mother's family, native Texans, was made up of carpenters, railroad men (there was a prominent roundhouse in Trinity), but her father was Postmaster of the town for many years. We lived in Trinity until I was seven. The world of that town, its countryside, its folk, its speech and superstitions and fable, was stamped into my senses during those first seven years of my life; and I spent the first twelve years of my writing life reporting it and fabricating it in short fiction. In my seventh year we moved to Shreveport, Louisiana, lived there a year, thence to Houston. I was educated, from the third grade, in that city: grammar school, Junior High School, High School, Rice University. As a child I was quick and scared; serving, secretly unsettled; imaginative and nervous and sensual. When I reached Sam Houston High School, I thought surely I would be a composer, actor, dancer, singer, fantastico. My mother and father were embarrassed by such ambitions. Nevertheless, I found a way to study dancing, music composition, singing, clandestinely. When this was found out by my parents, who were outraged by the extents of my determination, I did not run away from home to a city. I decided to go underground at home, and write. No one could know that I was doing that. It was my own. This was in my sixteenth year, and what I wrote was lyrical, melancholy, yearning, romantic and sentimental. Above all, it was homesick — and written at home.

College for me was intolerable. I hated the classes, the courses, the students. I wanted to make up new things, not "study" what had already been made. In my Junior year, the thunderstrike came. I discovered Shakespeare, Chaucer, Milton, Yeats, Joyce, the French Symbolists, Flaubert, Turgenev, Balzac, Melville, Hawthorne. I was at literature, insatiable, for the next three years, reading, and writing under the glow and turmoil of what I was reading. Suddenly — it seemed — I had accomplished the Masters Degree in Comparative Literature (1939). I had been writing plays and stories, and in my Junior and Senior years I took all the prizes in both forms.

At the end of the war, I went to New Mexico (El Prado, above Taos) and began to write from myself. It was clear to me now: I saw my life as a writing life, a life of giving shape to what happened, of searching for meanings, clarification, Entirety. It was my Way: expression in words. From then on, I managed to write, with little or no money, with growing distinction — which, I have come to see, brings little usable reward — awards, honors, little money. What I wanted was to make splendor. What I saw, felt, knew was real, was more than what I could make of it. That made it a lifetime task, I saw that. All forms of writing excite me and pain me and labor me; but the printed word, the Book — especially the short narrative form — most challenges and most frees me.

*W.G.*

## WORKS ABOUT WILLIAM GOYEN

Bachelard, Gaston. *The Poetics of Space*. New York: Orion Press, 1964.

Breit, Harvey. "Talk with William Goyen." *New York Times Book Review*. September 10, 1950, p. 12.

Curtius, Ernst Robert. "Zum Erstlingswerk sines jungen Amerikaners." *Neue Schweizer Bundschau*, Hft 11 (1952), pp. 669-675.

Dommergues, Pierre. *Les Ecrivains Americans D'Aujourd'hui*. Paris: Presses Universitaires De France, 1965.

——. *Les USA: A La Reserche de Leur Identite Recontres avec 40 Ecrivains Americains*. Paris: Grasset, 1967.

Gossett, Louise Y. *Violence in Recent Southern Fiction*. Durham: Duke University Press, 1965.

Hoffman, Frederick. *The Art of Southern Fiction*. Carbondale: Southern Illinois University Press, 1967.

Lucazean, Michel. "Surrealism in William Goyen." Diss. Bordeaux, 1963.

Mauriac, Claude. "Decouverte de William Goyen." *Preuves*, No. 40 (1954), pp. 85-87.

Mohrt, Michel. Preface to "Le Coq Blanc." *Le Table Ronde*, No. 63 (1953), pp. 53-55.

Nin, Anais. *The Novel of the Future*. New York: Macmillan, 1966.

Peden, William. *The American Short Story*. Boston: Houghton Mifflin, 1964.

Phillips, Robert. "Samuels and Samson: Theme and Legend in 'The White Rooster.' " *Studies in Short Fiction*, 6 (1969), 331-333.

——. "The Romance of Prophecy: Goyen's *In A Farther Country*." *Southwest Review*, 56 (1971), 213-221.

Stern, Daniel. "On William Goyen's The House of Breath." *Rediscoveries: Informal Essays in Which Well-Known Novelists Rediscover Neglected Works of Fiction by One of Their Favorite Authors*. Ed. David Madden. New York: Crown, 1971. pp. 256-261.

Sühnel, Rudolf. "Die Wiederentdeckung des Wunderbaren: William Goyen zum Gruss anlässlich seines Deutschlandbesuches." *Die Neueren Sprachen*, Heft 6 (1962), pp. 249-255.

## WORKS BY WILLIAM GOYEN

*Ghost and Flesh*. New York: Random House, 1952.

*In a Farther Country*. New York: Random House, 1955.

*The Collected Stories of William Goyen*. New York: Doubleday, 1972.

*The Faces of Blood Kindred*. New York: Random House, 1960.

*The Fair Sister*. New York: Doubleday, 1963.

*The House of Breath*. New York: Random House, 1950.

*Selected Writings*. New York: Random House-Bookworks, 1974.

*Another Man's Son*. New York: Doubleday, 1974.

*A Book of Jesus*. New York: Doubleday, 1973.

In addition to the novels and stories listed above, William Goyen has published reviews, articles, and poems in a variety of periodicals and has written and had produced plays for both the stage and television.

*from The House of Breath*

*WHAT is it the wind seeks, sweeping among the leaves, prowling round and round this house, knocking at the doors, and wailing in the shutters?*

O Charity! Every frozen morning for awhile in early winter you had a thin little winter moon slung like a slice of a silver Rocky Ford cantaloupe over the sawmill; and then I would go out to the well in the yard and snap off the silver thorns of ice from the pump muzzle and jack up the morning water and stand and look over across the fairy fields at you where you lay like a storybook town, and know that on all the little wooden roofs of houses there was a delicate trail of lacelike rime on the shingles. Then all the chickens and guineas of Charity would be crowing and calling and all the cattle lowing, and the Charity dogs barking (all with a sound that china animals might make if they could crow or call or low), and in that crystal and moonhaunted moment I would stand, dazzling in the first sunray of morning, and wonder what would ever happen to us all.

And on a spring Saturday you would be sitting there in your place in Texas "grinnin like a Chessy Cat" as Aunty said, so happy and hopping with all the people come in from the fields and farms to handle you and claim you and gather round in you—there was Glee Ramey and there was Sweet Climpkins and Sing Stovall and Ola Stokes, the music teacher

("One day a little bubble will break in your throat, honey, and then you'll have a beautiful voice. Just wait for the little bubble."), and all the Grants, who had to ford White Rock Creek to get in from their blackland farm—and families all standing together here and there or carrying out oats and feed cartons of Pet's Milk from the Commissary.

And in the still, clear dusks I remember especially a voice that sounded in you, Charity, resounding as in a cistern, calling "Swimma -a-a! Swimma -a-a-a! Come in 'fore dark!"— Aunty calling Sue Emma, my cousin and her daughter (no voice calling this name can ever call back Sue Emma to that fallen splendid house, and it grows dark. But Sue Emma, dancing or hunching in the dark, grinding in her own glitter's ashes, might hear a calling voice within her that does not answer back). All my life since, in any place and for no reason at all, sometimes at dusk I will suddenly hear a voice calling "Swimma -a-a! Swimma -a-a-a! Come in 'fore dark!"; and wish we were all together in Charity again.

You had a little patch of woods behind the house that I remember. It had bearded trees that clicked and ticked and cracked and cheeped and twittered and lichen grew on an ancient fence like an old old sheep's coat; and stroking it with my hand once made me feel how old and lusterless and napworn you might be, Charity, and all the people in you, just as Aunty said. But to see an old live oak drop a single young little leaf twinkling to the ground was to know that there was still the shining new thing of myself in the world and I would be filled with some passion for something, bigger than Aunty's hopelessness, bigger than Granny Ganchion's agony, than all Charity—until suddenly I would hear the groaning of the cisternwheel back at the house, calling me back, and I would go.

You were such a place of leaves, Charity; and I think the first time I was ever aware of you as any place in the world was in a deep and sad and heavy autumn. Then you seemed to have been built of leaf and twig and bark, as a bird's nest is woven and thatched together, and had been used and used until you were withered; then you were shaken and thrown down into these ruins. All the summer of anything that had ever touched or known you seemed despoiled and was rubble that autumn, and I suddenly knew myself as something, moving and turning among these remnants. Oh all the leaves I have known in you, Charity!—the shining leathery castor-bean leaves, with the chickens cool under them in the summer or sheltered from the rain (oh the sound of the rain on the castorbean leaves, how forever after Folner's funeral that sound reminded me of the funeral). And the lace and grace of chinaberry leaves in a summer breeze; and those of the vines that had a name I did not know and hung, full of bees or busy hummingbirds all after the little sweet white bloom on it, over the long front gallery of the house. Then of course the live-oak leaves, that were flaked over Charity Riverbottom; and muscadine leaves and sycamore leaves and the leaves on go-to-sleep flowers. (In the autumn of one year, every leaf that had ever hung on any Charity tree in spring and summer lay fallen upon the ground and I moved and turned through the wreckage like an unhung leaf that would not lie down nor wither.)

In you, Charity, there stands now, as in the globed world of my memory there glimmers the frosted image of it, blown by all these breaths, the fallen splendid house, sitting on the rising piece of land, out of which all who lived and lost in it have gone, being dispossessed of it; by death, by wandering, by turning away. And the house appears, now, to be an old old monument in an agony of memory of us, its ruined friezes of remains, full of our speech, holding our things that speak out after us as they once spoke into us, and waiting for one of us to give it back its language and so find his own. (But I think how our worlds—like this house—hold us within them like an idea they might be having or like dreams they are dreaming, where our faces are unreal, worn blurred stone faces of ancient metopes of kin, caught in soundless shapes of tumult, wrestling with invasion of some haunted demon race, half-animal, half-angel—O agony of faces without features like faces in fogs of dreams of sorrow and horror, worn holes of mouths opened, calling cries that cannot be heard, saying what words, what choked names of breath that must be heard.) And to find out what we are, we must enter back into the ideas and the dreams of worlds that bore and dreamt us and there find, waiting within worn mouths, the speech that is ours. For now in this autumn when all the young are ceaselessly walking up and down under the falling trees, trying to make themselves real, I have walked and walked among the leaves that lie like lost claws clutching the earth that fed them, weaving and winding myself to myself, binding the lost leaf back to the tree. For all that is lost yearns to be found again, re-made and given back through the finder to itself, speech found for what is not spoken.

$\mathcal{B}$EHOLD the house . . .

Now ruin has passed over all that fallen splendid house and done ruin's work on it. Now, ruin (of childhood) returning to ruin, come, purged of that bile and gall of childhood (into the empty purity of memory), come through the meadow called Bailey's Pasture that is spun over with luminous dandelions like a million gathered shining heads, through random blooming mustard and clover and bitter-weeds, over the grown-over path that was a short-cut to town when there was no circus or revival tent there. Pass one brown spotted cow folded there (remember her name as a calf was Roma and a good ride) and munching the indestructible bitterweed cud of time, and pass around the silent laboring, nervous civilization of an anthill that swarms and traffics on and on beyond the decline of splendid houses or the fall of broken cisternwheels. The slow grinding of cud, even and measured, the twinkling, red, timeless quarry of ants and the eternal, unalterable cycle of flowers—first the white, then the pink, then red to blue to purple and finally to sunflower yellow—round and round, turning and turning, moving and moving: they mock the crooked mile that families walk, suffering and failing and passing away, over their crooked stile, into a crooked Beulah Land.

If you come this way about this time of a time, through

Bailey's Pasture, you will then come to and have to cross over the warped, rusted railroad tracks of the MKT, called Katy Railroad; and, having crossed the rails, you will behold before you this house. You think you hear a voice—from the shuttered window? From the front gallery? From the cellar, the loft?—murmuring, "But who comes here, across the pasture of bitterweeds, wading in through the shallows, home?"

If you be Beryben Ganchion you have returned after a long long time and too late. For your mother, Malley Ganchion, has gone blind from cataracts that kept her half-blind for such a long time, sitting by the closed shutter in this house, along, waiting for you to come back.

If you be Sue Emma Starnes, you are too late, too; and if you be any other, then you have returned for all of them, for all their sakes, come to rummage and explore, in your hour, and find a meaning, and a language and a name.

Open the rusted iron gate and step across the sticker-burrs blooming in the grass, go round past the rotted tire where the speckled canna used to live and turn towards the cisternwheel that does not turn. See the cistern, rusted and hollow and no water in it, and the wheel of the windmill wrecked and fallen and rats playing over the ruin. The wheel is like an enormous metal flower blighted by rust. Bend down to touch the fallen petals and, bending, hear the grinding groan of the wheel that begins to turn again in your brain of childhood, rasping the overtone of loneliness and moaning the undertone of wonder. Remember how it rose up on long legs out of the round, deep, lidded stock tub, and remember once when the lid was left off how the child of a Negro washwoman (recall her poking, head wrapped in a scrap of red bandanna, the steaming black iron pot full of Starnes and

Ganchion clothes) climbed up and fell into the tub and was drowned and how the cows come to drink bellowed to find its corpse.

Now the wheel lies in a grotesque ruin by the rusted and empty tub, and weed grows up between its metal petals (and sunflowers, crooking over after the sun, mock because they turn) and rats scuttle over the wreckage. It lies like the emblazonment of a fallen house, blazoned by rat's scratches and rust engravings, the intaglios carved in by decay; and, vanquished and defiled like the coat of arms of Starnes and Ganchion, it lies unturned by the wind that brushes against it but cannot turn it, useless and disempowered. (Once its turning was like a silver burning in the autumn sunlight, flashing and turning in its gyre so that wind in it meant water and families lived by wind, as a sailed ship. And if the wind came from the direction of the sawmill it bore and scattered over the house the piney pollen of sawdust; and if from the direction of the river bottomlands, the scents of pines glistening far from the hot inferno of kilns, and the sweet breath of the Charity Riverwoods.

Often I stood, boy blown in the wind that blew upon the cisternwheel and turned it, in an autumn dusk, a big hand holding mine, and watched the whirling of the wheel. I felt myself a steady fixed point on the earth round which a whirling gathered and spun as a center. Then it was that I seemed to be no one, to belong to no one (he holding my hand) and suddenly beholding the russet light of the turning sumach tree in the pasture (pulled down and stolen from all light by that terrible winter's long ropes of solid ice), I thought, *O I am leaf and I am wind and I am light. Something in the world links faces and leaves and rivers and woods and wind together and makes of them a string of*

*medallions with all our faces on them, worn forever round
our necks, kin.*

Dare you go into the house? Go, entering through the
back door (out of which you used to throw the water from
the washstand to the chickens gathered waiting for it. Oh the
mournful mewling of Aunty's young broilers waiting at the
steps for you in the mornings or at dusks when you would
wash at the washstand: they haunt you, the calls of the
broilers, their plaints and plaintive whines in the yard) which
opens on the screened-in breezeway. There seems some hand,
big and broken-knuckled, waiting at the door taking your
hand to lead you.

On this breezeway in the summer afternoons she held
the flyswatter like a scepter and Uncle Jimbob sat, poorly
and silent, on a little barrel, and all of them, the Cousins and
Aunts and Uncles and other kin, just sitting there with
nothing to do, nowhere to go, nothing to dress up for, just
sitting. And then, hearing wheels on the road and running to
the kitchen window, she shouted "The gypsies!", and all of
them gathered at the windows, watching the bright gypsies
jingle down the road, bright and quick and going someplace,
and none of them saying a word, all of them gathered at the
windows, looking through the windows.

Her drinking well was right in the house at the end of
the long back porch next to the indoor privy (there was a
crooked one outside beyond the chickens, but in it were
hornets). This was the only magic thing, the dark, enchanted
well that held the beautiful voice prisoner, down below the
shimmering water. When you cried down, "Hello! hello!", it
answered back only, "O! . . . O!", in a wailing young girl's
voice.

When Uncle Jimbob had to clean the well he would

draw out all the water and lower you down into the darkness on a little wooden sling of a seat. You dreamt of it, and often—forever—(for you had been so bred as a well-creature, brother to the bucket, lowered empty and pulled up full and brimming clear to be drunk down by waiting thirst—child of wheel and cistern-child, with gift of turning) felt the terrible descent of alienation from face and voice and light into empty, lightless loneliness (but O Granny Ganchion, joined to you, below); and knew, that once you were pulled up (by whom, what hand?) into light and warmth again, you would somewhere in you be changed by the well-terror and committed to make it known to those on the summer breezeway as vision, for all their sakes. For each time you ascended—by hard will, by choice, by courage, you had a responsibility to the vision of descent. Down on the cold sand floor of the well you crouched, cold and trembling, and heard the mysterious voices beyond the well (as you heard them from your pallet often, whispering in the next room) talking in an easy summer afternoon: Aunty's and Malley's and Granny's and Swimma's and the others', and wondered, alien there, if you would ever be joined to them again—or if you were, whether you could ever really tell them what your terror in the well had been; or heard the voices round the blue hole far above, voices of the gathered faces round the rim calling down "Boy! Boy! Can you hear your name?"

(The wheel is broken at the cistern, the rope at the well is raveled and rotten, the bucket is rusted and leaky; and there is never a hand on the windlass now.)

And in the front yard in the late summer afternoons when the children played barefoot upon the sticker-burrs, all her kin sat rocking round her on the porch and she spat snuff into the front yard and rocked and said, "This is an old house. That was pore Mama and Papa's room there. I remember pore Mama and Papa sleeping in that front room where Malley and Walter Warren and Jessy and Berryben live now when all of us was children."

And the children in the front yard running barefooted over the stickerburrs, singing "Go in and out the windows, go in and out the windows, go in and out the windows, for we have gained this day."

Or, in the game of Statue, all the Starnes and Ganchion young thrown into frozen poses, bent-over mourning shapes or vain or heroic arabesques—so that in memory they seem like a pavilion of ruined statuaries. (Folner even then would cheat a pose into some careless, blase stance, but he could not ransom his face.)

The little train would go by in front of the house and stop all rocking and any game and where, where was it going? And who was the wild-faced man in the dirty cap who waved the gloved-black hand from the engine as it passed? And what was he trying to say to all of them, to the children playing games in the big front yard round the speckled canna and the big ones rocking on the long gallery in the swing and wicker rockers? Here they sat and ran as he passed, and oh who *was* he, this leering, magical, terrible man who waved the great gloved-black hand at them from the little engine as it passed, going where? coming from where? Oh they said it was going to Riverside, but that train was going *everywhere*.

"And oh," Aunty said, "we ain't got a chanct, we ain't got a chanct in this world. Jimbob's down in the back and got hemorrhoids and a stone in his bladder and cain't carpenter or work at the roundhouse or even lift a good size squash; and the garden's dry and burning up in the burnin sun and we cain't buy feed for the cows and chickens and I

don't know what we'll ever do, just set here on this porch
and rock and spit until we die one day and be buried by our
pore relations. And Swimma finishin high school next year
and then where does she go and what does she do? If she goes
wild like that Willadean Clegg I'd rather see her dead, I
declare to you all and to the good Lord I'd rather see her
dead. But I can see it comin. Ought to have her a business
course in Palestine, but who on earth can afford to pay for
the kind of course she needs at Miz Cratty's Select Business
College in Palestine? And Maidie marryin Fred that runs a
streetcar in Dallas and who can live off the money they pay
you to run a streetcar in Dallas? And Malley and Walter
Warren unhappy and little Jessy sickly—and this infernal little
town of Charity dead and rottin away with only the Ralph
Sandersons havin the money and all the rest of us pore as
nigras and our teeth bad and my side hurtin day and night
with the change a life and no money to see a specialist in
Dallas (Jimbob, Jimbob, the pigs is in the peapatch again, but
don't run. Walk, Jimbob, mind your back). My Lord, guess
we'll all die in a pile right here, with the pigs in the peapatch
and nobody carin, nobody carin.

"Why? On New Year's Day I cook my cabbage and
make my pillow slips."

"Aunty, why does the Widow Barnes just sit on her
porch?"

Oh all the porches in the little town had them rocking
on them, sitting, sitting; and the crops burning up under the
burning sun and the teeth going bad and stones in the
bladders and the town rotting away and no place to go, no
place to go.

The Ku Klux Klan went riding riding. You saw the fiery
cross on Rob Hill in the summer nighttime and you knew

some poor crazy riverbottom Negro was going to burn, was going to run shrieking down Main Street in tar and feathers.

"Aunty, Aunty, what is that noise by the woodstove?"

"Be still, Boy. It's only the rats in your Aunty's woodbox."

"Oh the sad sad days when all of us was young," she said, and spat and rocked. "You know when Mama passed on, she left me all her old crockery. There was some big pitchers with roses handpainted on them. And then the old nigra Mary Bird who cleaned for Mama for years just took them all, sayin they was rightfully hers because she was the only one that ever was kind to Mama and rightfully deserved them. Everthing we ever had is gone. What they don't steal away from us we lose by drout or a plague or a rottin away. Life is hard and only sufferin and it does no good to any of us and how we ever bear it I don't know. But we have it to do and we've got to be strong about it and try not to be blue about it and go on in trial and tribylation. But how life changes and the things that happen to us in this world are like stories to be read and I declare the great God don't even know sometimes the dreadful things that happen to us; and oh Boy, Boy, let me push back the hair from your eye. Goin to be wrinkled as old man Nay down by the sawmill, worst suit a hair I ever saw. Come to me—lemme roach back ya hair. The Ganchions are the blight of Charity, and I know it, worse than boll weevils, worse than a pest a hoppers, the Devil incarnit, despise the day we all come here from Sour Lake, us rawsin bellies; Charity ruined us. Don't frown so, Boy, don't worry so; commere, lemme roach back the hair from ya eye . . ."

"Aunty, Aunty, who am I? Who are we? What kin are we all to each other?"

"The gingerbread man he ran and ran; and melted as he ran. On the nose of the fox he melted down into the tears of the fox that ran . . . When we was all in Sowlake with Mama and Papa, runnin in the fields and playin in the wagon it seemed like nothin ever could happen to any of us. (Papa played a jew's-harp on the screenporch in the evenins.) When Walter Warren married Malley we all nearly died, I tell you, nearly killed us. That was the beginnin of the whole trouble; then we come to Charity, then the Starnes come into this house, one by one, right in on us, till we 'uz all here together. Ever year got harder and harder, drouts come and floods come and children come; the whole world was changing, preachers said the end a the world was comin, wickedness everwhere and sickness everwhere, and no money.

"Maidie was so sweet and quiet, always minded me and never give me one lick a trouble. When the Revival meetin was acrost in Bailey's Pasture we'd go and there sang the best quartet I ever heard in my life, the Sunshine Boys; and Fred Suggs was in it, a tenor with a beautiful solo voice. When the Sunshine Boys sang, *Man of the world, why stand ye idle all the day? Look up to Christ, he will forgive, your sins he'll wash away! Then be prepared to meet thy God and of the feast partake; The King of Kings is ruler there, he guards the golden gate!* this was just about the peacefulest thing in the world; and when Fred Suggs would chime in with his beautiful tenor voice: *Is there anyone here who is not prepared to pass through the golden gate? Be ready, for soon the time will come to enter the golden gate. Don't let it be said, too late, too late, to enter the golden gate. Be ready, for soon the time will come, to enter the golden gate.*

"Well, Fred Suggs was just the finest boy, we brought him across the tracks to Sunday dinner and he and Maidie picked a watermelon from the patch and we had it and then they went walkin down the tracks afterwards. I knew they wanted to marry and in the Fall Fred Suggs come back to Charity and they married and went away to Dallas. It nearly killed me to pack her suitcase, but I waved at them from the gate and they went on off to Dallas. Pore Maidie, she cries ever night for Charity and all of us in this house, and I wish she could come back, the city's no place for Maidie, no place for pore pineywoods folks, Maidie's no city girl, never was farther than White Rock Bridge on Fourth of July picnics before she went to Dallas. She don't even know her neighbors, they work all day, and on Sunday she takes the children to Sunday School and they they ride the streetcar to the end a the line and back. Sometimes she goes to town to Kress a little, but that's about all. The time they made me come to Dallas to see the dentist was awful, firewagons howlin their sireens ever minute, those streetcars grindin day and night, just couldn't stand it. "This town's burning down and they're all killin each other, I can't sleep or set still and I'm goin back home,' I said; and declared I uz comin back to Charity. Said I'd order my teeth from Sears (certainly wouldn't have Doctor Stokes in Charity to make my teeth, that drunkard; he's ruined ever mouth in Charity).

"But pore little Maidie in that duplex in that city; I wish she'd come back here. Wish all of em would come on back here and we could have our reunions that we used to have when all the Starnes ud come in from the woods. Never saw so much squash and yella-legged chicken in your life, all the young Starnes not a one under six feet, and the pretty, timid girls—where have they all gone? I tell you the Devil walked in the riverbottoms—and cussed this town.

"I just want to set right here in this house, don't want

to see nobody, don't care if they all never come here again, just want to set here in this old rotten house until I die. Never had nothin, never will have nothin, none of us ever had a chanct and I don't care any more, be glad when I die, wish I'd hurry up, then it'll be all over with."

Oh you ain't got a chanct, you ain't got a chanct in this world. You are down in the back and got hemorrhoids and a stone in your bladder and you can't carpenter or work at the roundhouse and the garden's dry and burnin up in the burnin sun and you can't buy feed for the cows and chickens and I don't know what you'll ever do, just sit there on the porch and rock and spit and die one day and be buried by your poor relations. And the infernal little town dead and rottin away and all of you poor as niggers and your teeth bad and your sides hurtin day and night and no money to see a doctor in Dallas.

"(And Jimbob, Jimbob, the pigs is in the peaptach but don't run, walk, Jimbob. Mind your back, Jimbob. My Lord guess we'll all die in a pile right here with the pigs in the peapatch and nobody carin.)"

Nobody carin.


Now a spider lives unbothered in the doormat that never knows a pawing foot upon it.

There is the kitchen gathered around the great worn woodstove. A faded map is still tacked on the wall. You hear the mice kicking in the turned-over oatmeal. And you hear the wind that lopes like a spectral rider round and round the house, whirls down the flues and chutes into the woodstove and thrashes the ashes and blows a wild little horn in the hollows of the stove. Then you hear a melody from a farther room and it is the wind blowing a tune in the closed shutter in the room where Malley Ganchion lived on like a mouse in the house after all the others had gone, hoping some redemption for them all would come.

Some appetite waits and lurks in the world, you remark; it is some great hunger, insect and rodent and decay hunger. This seems suddenly to be a law of the universe. Insect, mold, rat, rust, death—all wait for and get the human plunder in the end, to carry the carrion away. The vultures of this greed hover and plane over us all our lives, waiting to drop down. The leaf has its caterpillar, the stalk mildew and the worm lies crooked in the bud. And observe the little white lice, dandruff in the golden head of the marigold, the gall chancres and fistulas on the rosebush. See the shale of fly carcasses in the spiderwebs, of caught hornets and flying ants, wings folded like a closed fan (the dead of this house lie fastened in what web, stretched over what blue Kingdom?), bits of wings and antennae, all debris. The dirtdobbers' knobs of mud, lathed round and whorled smooth, hang like many lightless lanterns—because there is no hand to knock them down. The insects have taken over—we fight them back all our lives, but in the end they come victoriously in, our inheritors. Look in the corners, under things—find the little purewhite puffs and tents in which some whiskery thing lives, find the thousand-legs and stinkbugs and doodlebugs and Junebugs, find fantastic bugs with shielded backs and delicate marks and brilliant colors and designs. See a caught mouse in a trap—set by what futile, mocked hand?—rotted to a frail skull and a vertebra. And see over the boards of the faded floor the Sienese lines of tracks and roads and tunnels and cross-hatched marks and trails. In the bins and cannisters are weevils; the roaches, unmolested, are grown big. The legged armies have come into this house. This is the slow eating away—mold and canker and mildew and must, gall and parasite, lice and little speckled ticks and grooved worms. In a corner of the pantry (where you often ran to hide from old Mr. Hare, passing in his rumbling wagon calling "paa-ahs! paa-ahs!") discover a ruined still life of left vegetables, whiskered and leprosied, and rotted fruit spotted with pustules and the stippled fuzz of fungus. (You remember the glassy picture in the dining room, where you ate on Sundays, that was of a sad dead blue duck dangling down a golden-flecked and purple-speckled head—with staring eyes that watched you eat—and pears and peaches round him; and feel that picture's ruin before you.)

And all so quiet is this eating away, except for the wind that winds a mummy cloth around the fallen splendid house delivered to its inheritors.

So this is why when often as you came home to it, down the road in a mist of rain, it seemed as if the house were founded on the most fragile web of breath and you had blown it. Then you thought it might not exist at all as built by carpenters' hands, nor had ever; and that it was only an idea of breath breathed out by you who, with that same breath that had blown it, could blow it all away.

FOLNER was sad and cheap and wasted, a doll left in the rain, a face smeared and melted a little, soft and wasted and ruined. Where did he go when he crept away in the nighttime, staying sometimes for two or three days, then returning spent and wasted and ruined a little in his face?

(Now ruin returning to ruin (passion of Beast to Prince's peace) come, purged of that spleen and blood of passion (into the empty purity of peace), come through Bailey's Pasture (Beauty's changed Beast) over the railroad track and home—who had lapped with bestial tongue the riverwater at the river, the blood of creatures under his nailed claws and a salt tear dripping into the river. (He waits for the crashing of glass—alone in our most ultimate distresses we all wait for the crashing of glass when the glittering Redemption will rise, springing corruptible and purified from a pasture of bitter-weeds—O endless cycle of suffering that turns between Beast and Prince— and hears only the endless sound of the feet of the bird grinding upon leaves.) Ruin in the peace of afterpassion, peaceful and destroyed a little in the ruins of the jack-knife agony, the leaping shrimp-like flexions, in the collapse and debris of earthquake of kiss and trembling, himself a ground ruin, the hiss of finish whispering from the ruin like the aftersmoke over rubble: did he not know that ruin lay wound within the works of everything, for him?

That every constructed thing carried hidden in it the intricate greengolden wheels and chains of terror that turned for him? Did he not know that the house of breath and blood that held him promised only terror within every room, where terror would break out through some unconsidered door to chime its own plumed hour of irreversible doom upon him? He walked in the rime of the bog of the icebound bottomlands and heard, with beak of horn and horned nails, the bird of fire whose prey he was, chiming his terrible Midnight; his image in the rime of the bog is rainbow . . . He is Devil, he is Prince, he is Heartbreak. He is destiny of fire, he is ashes and cinders. He is artifice of breath, grinding in his own ruin's cinders under a blown, gray, bubbled moon of breath across a field of ash.)

He would come across town and through Bailey's Pasture home to us through the bitterweeds with dock and wild buckwheat in his blonde hair, and below his eyes the blue rims of circles, the color of eggplant, would shine on his flushed cheeks—the Prince of Peace returneth—beast had spring into Prince in the riverbottoms, agony of vision married to agony of body in the rain, vision eating body, flesh become word. He said—and now I understand—*"Behold this gift of darkness this house has given me and I give you; I have stolen your light away. We are, and never will be. In all your sunshines if you can remember one day any darknesses, that was me drawing you . . . I have left Word in the darkness for you, the Word that was my flesh; all darkness proclaims my Word; listen in the darkness and you will hear it."*

He chose a show to go away with, finally, out of East Texas because I think it was the only bright and glittering thing in the world he could find. Of all the ways and things in the world, he chose a show, with acrobats and lights and spangles. Because he couldn't bear the world without a song and dance and a burnished cane. He was wild like a creature, the way he crept as if he went on paws like an animal out of the brush, a kind of hunted, creeping thing in his gait. He was for the beautiful evil world and he let it ravage him to ash, he gave his life for it. (Was *he* what Christy hunted for in the woods, going with his birdbag and his gun and returning with bird's blood on him and a chatelaine of slain birds girdled round his hips?) He went all the way. He knew what he was and endured it all the way, to the bitter bitter end, burned down to ash by it, charred down to clinker. (I embrace him now, against this wall in the rain.)

They told about the trunks of costumes that came back to Charity after he took sleeping pills at midnight in a hotel in San Antonio—they said he was coming home from New York City and had got that far, lingered on the very edge of Charity in San Antone but couldn't come on in home—all the trunks up in the loft, filled with rhinestones and spangles and boa-feathers and holding the wicked smell of greasepaint. I rummaged there as if I thought somewhere I might suddenly come upon some explanation of his mystery.

Brave and noble, Folner? Clean and fine? Boy Scouts and the Epworth League and all that, Folner? Pshaw! You didn't want to flicker around East Texas, you wanted to *blaze* in the world, to sparkle, to shine, to glisten in the great evil world. You wanted tinsel and tinfoil and spangle and Roman candle glamor, to be gaudy and bright as a plaster ruby and a dollar diamond. Was that right? Of course not. Wrong? What *is* wrong?

"Who has a *choice*, really?" you said.

All of it was wrong from the beginning, from the corrupted foetus, the poisoned womb, from the galled cradle (endlessly rocking for you and me, for you and me).

You were tinsel all the way, beautiful boy Folner, all the rotten way. Once I said, building a chicken coop, "I want to make this *right.*"

"Nothing is made right around here, Boy," you said. "Everything is crooked and warped and twisted."

And walked, lost and cheaply grieved, away; and I wondered what you meant.

When your corpse came back to Charity from San Antonio that deep and leaf-haunted autumn, Folner, they embalmed it at Jim Thornton's Funeral Establishment (which was also a cleaning and pressing shop when nobody was dead). There was a gray hearse. All of us went to the Grace Methodist Church and the Starnes and the Ganchions filled up two pews. We sang "Beaulah Land" (You would have loved that . . . "for I am drinking from the fountain that never shall run dry (praise God!); I'm feasting on the manna of a bountiful supply . . ."). A few women kept fainting. Aunty sat hating you, even dead. Even laid in a coffin she despised you like a snake. Granny Ganchion sat like a sick bird, humped and bitten, and gazed into your cheap coffin. Oh her hands!—bony and knotted at the knuckles—how she moved them round her goitered throat like a starved woman's. (Do you know what she wore, Folner? A great yellow hat with a boafeather round it, and on her neck was a pair of rubyred beads. What voices were howling round in her head as she sat there, gazing at you in your cheap coffin?) Your brother Christy sat out in front of the church in the car, would not come in, sullen and wretched. As we marched by your coffin to look in at you for the last time, I saw your wasted doll-in-the-rain face and I thought I could hear you whisper to me, "Make it gay, Boy, make it bright, Boy!" And no one in that whole Grace Methodist Church, or in all of Charity, or in the whole wide world but you and I knew I dropped a little purple spangle into your cheap coffin as I passed by. It was a little purple spangle stolen from a gypsy costume in one of your trunks in the loft. You loved it! It was put in the earth with you.

At your funeral there was a feeling of doom in the Grace Methodist Church, and I sat among my kin feeling dry and throttled in the throat and thought we were all doomed—who are these, who am I, what are we laying away, what splendid, glittering, sinful part of us are we burying like a treasure in the earth?

(The Grace Methodist Church had started out underground. There had been only enough money to build a basement with, and for several years we went down steps into the Church, like a cellar, and had a meeting. In summer it was full of crickets; and often, tired of the singing, we would go outside and sit on the steps and watch the summer toadfrogs leap after and lick in the crickets. But when old Mr. Ralph J. Sanderson, the owner of the sawmill and terror of Negroes, had died, he had left enough money for a ground floor and some colored glass windows and these were added as a memorial to him.)

There were about thirty rows of pews and the Starnes and Ganchions occupied two of them at the funeral. Charity came and filled the rest.

On the raised platform in front under a bare arch were the folding chairs where the choir sat, and to the right of the chairs was the piano. Nina Dot Dooley was the pianist. (She said it peeanist and always ended even the most austere anthem with rolling chords, finishing up on a very high and tinkling treble note with her little finger that was arched over with a dinner ring displayed upon it. She had an orange, spotted face.) In the center of the altar, which was only the barest hint of an altar, stood one spare crooked candle in a goldplated holder: the cause of the schism in the church that finally broke the old and the new factions apart and caused Brother Hildebrandt to form the Church Foursquare and lead his followers with him.

A quartet was sitting straight in the choirloft—it was Mrs. Shanks (called Horseface by all the boys because she had black lips that peeled back off her two rows of large, square, roastingear teeth when she sang out); Miss Pearl Selmers, the alto and the only alto in the church with a trained voice and therefore in every duet or quartet, singing sadly and so faintly you could scarcely hear her; Mr. Bybee, the forced tenor, singing always eeeeeeeee with a quavering sound like a saw played; and Mr. Chuck Addicks, the little old bass.

(Once the Ku Klux Klan interrupted the sermon on Sunday to come marching down the center aisle in their sheets, terrifying the congregation who did not know who among them they might be coming after—but they had come in only to make a demonstration in favor of the preacher, of whom they approved, and to give a donation, wrapped in a white handkerchief, to the church. One of the sheets moved unevenly with a hobble and people knew it was Walter Warren Starnes.)

Then the quartet stood, rattling the folding chairs, and with great austerity sang "For his eye is on the sparrow, and I know he watcheth me . . ." (You were no sparrow in that coffin, Folner; you were a plumed and preened gorgeous bird, hatched in a borrowed nest, cuckolded, meant for some paradise garden.)

The sermon was a long and sad one. It told about all the

family, about your young life in Charity and your work in the Church. (Once you had stood, at ten, before the whole congregation and recited the books of the Bible first forwards, then backwards. You had been a bright boy. You had sinned. The Lord save your soul.)

I want to make a little speech upon the passing of this boy, the sermon said. We have lost a leaf from a beautiful old Charity tree (a leaf! a leaf!). A bright star has fallen over Charity (a star!). We have lost a jewel (a sequin! a rhinestone! a parure of great price!), a toy of the world (O Jack-in-the-Box!). This is a piece of the lavish gay world brought back to Charity black earth, the bitterweed pollen of the bitterweed of the world clings to his limbs brought home to this hive. (Green bee that gyres out of season over us, grown thus into what yield of bitterweed are we? Pollen to what cilia (spike in the horses' throat, death in the fowls' craw) of what green bee of gall?) We are burying the brightness of the world. We are burying like a foul thing in the dirt this twisted freak, like Sue Emma's two little monsters, little slobbering freaks with bloated watermelon heads. Sue Emma's sins (and every day they'd come and measure and measure—their head was like Granny Ganchion's vile goiter, round and swollen and strutted with purple veins big as a chicken's intestines). O precious shard of the Old Mother Lode that we bury! Old Mother Lode, ore of what dark cursed vein?

Songs went through my head, Folner, as I sat there, songs I had known where, when? "O had I wings of Noah's dove, I'd fly away to the one I love . . ." "One day you goin come and call my name . . ." "My love went away on a long long train . . ." And the little verse, piping itself out in my brain, over and over . . . "It was just a little doll, dears, brought in from the fields and the rain; its hair not the least

bit curled, dears; and its arm trodden off by the cows. And
its face all melted away . . ." And the tale of the gingerbread
man who ran and ran and melted away as he ran . . . And the
mournful little tune that a child could blow on a petunia; and
the words of the hymn "O Love That Wilt Not Let Me
Go . . ."

"When I was young," the voices howled round in
Granny Ganchion your mother's head as she sat there gazing
at you in your cheap pink coffin, "I loved gems and jewels
and would almost steal to have a colored ring to glisten on
my finger, just like a Gypsy. We are burying here the glassy
part of me. O me . . . desire faileth; it is the burden of the
grasshoppers. *There is a fountain filled with blood, drawn
from Immanuel's veins; And sinners plunged beneath that
flood lose all their guilty stains* . . . Sure we had nothing in
Charity but Beulah Land to hope for and wait for—but how
could that help? That wasn't enough while we waited. The
church cheated us, Brother Ramsey cheated us. I had to
burrow down *under* it all like a quick mole to have any life.
Don't think I don't know all this. Now there Follie, lay still,
lay still. Remember when I couldn't keep you quiet on a
pallet in the summer afternoons when you would have to
take your nap? This is the last pallet, little Follie, a pallet for
good. Lay still on it, child. (There's old Miz Van come to
your funeral—she brought you the first present you ever got
in this world—a pitcher of cold buttermilk the morning you
were born. Fly in the buttermilk Lula Lula . . .)

"What does he say, Brother Ramsey, in his talking, in
his sermon? He is condemning Follie to hellfire. The Lord
hath hung this millstone upon my neck, and I know what for
and I have never told. It is a lavalier of wickedness. It is the
enormous rotten core of Adam's Apple. But I have had my

life in my time—some way . . ."

(You knew lips, how they move to make their words;
and the gimaces of faces when you were yelled at were
sometimes so grotesque that you dreamt of them, strained
and veined and goggle-eyed—and in your dreams the faces
were only making faces at you and not saying anything.

You came to hear only the voices in your head. All the
world beyond you was hushed as though some turning of a
great wheel was stopped beyond you (but went on inside
you), and there remained only the silence of working mouths
on shifting faces—and there was only the babel of voices in
your head.

When desire failed you, you had nothing left but the
betrayal of desire (the moth-eaten coronation robes of
dethroned queens) and a pair of ruby beads given you once
by a dark alien youth who found you at a carnival and loved
you and stayed to love you longer and again. You would steal
away at night and run to him at the City Hotel and all the
town knew. It was said that Christy was this stranger's son
but no one ever proved it, for Christy was black-headed and
swarthy among the other towheads—but this could have been
the Indian blood that was supposed to be in the Ganchion
veins come out in him, you said.

Your father was a southern sea-captain with a wart on
the left side of his nose for lechery and by the time you were
fourteen he had shot dead two Negroes for not keeping their
place and calling him Cap'n.

You had had a hand upon your thigh in the church
choir that made you trill like a meadowlark, "Fling Wide the
Gates!"; and once while singing "Hear The Soft Whisper" at
communion when all the heads were bent, you received your
first baptism of joy—and had been Joy's sister ever since.)

And then, when the family started walking by your coffin, Folner, to look at your doll-in-the-rain face for the last time, Granny Ganchion flung herself into your coffin and tried to seize you to her, crying out in her carline voice, but you would not come up to her; and they pulled her away.

As we drove along (what Charity was not in the procession was standing watching us like a parade) a storm broke over us and scattered leaves. It was the first full devastation of Autumn.

We stood around the grave and they let you down in it while Brother Ramsey sprinkled rose petals. It seemed he was murmuring, "sawdust to sawdust," and that surely what was falling was sawdust from the planing mill. All around the graveyard there was the ruin of Summer, Summer's wreck and plunder. Weeds were rusty with seed and the zinnias were crumbling. And then all the members of the families fell upon each other, embracing and kissing and wailing and sharing their separate and secret tragedies; and for a moment at the Charity Graveyard there was a reunion of blood and a membership of kin over your grave (the odor of lilies and carnations gave me a sensuous, exotic elation that I was ashamed of). There was a kind of meekness and the relief felt in truce. Some took a flower from your grave and fought others to keep it—it was like a battle of fiends over a holy prize; and Aunt Malley came up in a trance and said to Cousin Lottie, "What kin are we all to each other, anyway?"

But the deaf old Mother, wise and bitter and skeptic, did not fall to the graveyard trickery and stood off to herself, gazing at your grave.

There seemed to be some misery over in the world. Some atonement, some ransom was paid for all of us, for all our Sins. Now, in due time and in right season, what resurrection of what spirit would assure us of the meaning of this death. Folner?

As we turned to go away and leave you in the graveyard, I looked back and discovered a tall and sorrowful stranger standing along by a crepemyrtle tree. It seemed he wanted to say something to me, that he was beckoning to me. But we got in our cars and drove away and he turned and watched us as we went away.

The next day there was a change in the whole world. There was a moon in the daytime like the pale, lashless lid of a drooping eye and it haunted the day. Then rain fell while the sun shone and the devil was beating his wife; birds flew in and over and away, as if bewildered (they knew), one of the hens crowed and a whirlwind got caught in the beantree and rattled the dry pods. I went out among the castorbeans and sat and heard the sad rain, like a faint weeping, dripping on the leaves.

Finally in the afternoon it seemed the whole earth died, dried up and faded and curled. Huge blood-green maple leaves drifted like lost wings in the wind. Hens moulted. Some amputation had happened in the world, some desperate surgery. The fantasy was finished; something crueler was beginning, hard and of agony. The winter was close and lay long and gray and leafless ahead. Something waited for me, now—a world of magic and witchcraft, the brute, haunted world of some nameless terrible beauty, whirling in the twilight glimmer of coming hope and hopelessness. (Who has not seen the gizzard-like birthmark on the luminous temple of the moon?)

Then as the day ended, in the terrifying sunset that was like the ends-of-the-world dusks I had dreaded so often, the rain fell golden in the distance and the golden rain fell over the sawmill, apotheosizing it, as if it had achieved some kind of victory.

You've been buried in Charity for a number of years, Follie, our Follie, and I am called back to the loft where your relics lie stored; and I am here among them rummaging for some answer. It is hard to be in the world and bone of your bone. Cry me out a name, which like a spangle cast out to me, I may carry out of this loft with me.

I come, bending low, into the loft. I had been here once before with Aunty to rummage for a picture of her mother, and when we found the picture it had one eye eaten out by some animal and looked hideous and staring and tormented.

Then I went again and again, with a heavy feeling of sin. I was looking for something *within myself* that might flower out in this warm, secret light, unfurl (I had in my mind the vermilion image of a paper Hallowe'en serpent that would unroll, splendid and quivering, when blown into) like a paper flower dropped in a bowl of water. I felt the excitement—the first I can remember—of discovery, like the feeling I had when I crept into forbidden books. (*Eugenics* was big and black and evil, hidden under the linens of the closet and there I first saw the picture of a woman with a window in her belly through which I could see a little, wound baby, all in a sac entwined by a mass of strings and cords.) I trembled in the loft.

Here in the loft, which is really your sepulchre, Folner, are many things of silence and dignity; and it seems that in them lie all the hope, all the future, in the riot of insects and rodents which are feeding on this storage of antiques.

There is a spinningwheel which spiders have mocked with glittering webs like doilies and lace valentines. There is an organ with a rat world in its insides, and rats' feet sift over the strings with the faintest prism tinkle like the death-knell of the delicate. On a sugarcane pole in a corner are strung old dresses and coats and, crumpled in a corner, is a Ku Klux Klan hood like a caved-in ghost. The clothes hanging in the purple loftlight are shredded by claws and streaked by rain and drenched in light and burned through by ceaseless rays of sunlight and moonlight and starlight. They are ripped by teeth and gnawing (almost as if in some kind of vengeance) and the tiny punctures of the mouths of ants and moths, as if the wearing of life had left some sweet syrup on them. A gray, diaphanous veil hangs like a web and spun so fine by age that it seems a veil of light. Because these garments have been so long diffused with light and lights—through many washings and drenchings—their colors have faded and the lights have dyed them delicate pale Light colors.

In an eave is a whole mosque of dirtdobber domes and globed hives of bees and the blown gray papiermache bags of wasps. Curtains of gossamer hang trembling purple and luminous. In this wreckage the insects and creatures have made their artifice and their order: frail mouth-built or cilia-built structures, envelopes and membranes and spun-out or spat-out fragile architecture, phantom and fantastic and terrifying.

The faded pine walls wear Wear like a fabric, a garment of speared and cometed and darted and spiraled grain, and grain designs like those on the sole of a foot; and lacunae of lucent amber resin; and serrated or glabrous surfaces: a landscape of figures of grotesque naked men and women among pools and hummocks and flumes; and there are fantastic scrawlings and lewd phalliforms of grain. On one wall there is a terrible water-mark figure like the huge claw of an enormous bird grappling over a long dried pool of blood.

There is an old cowboy hat felted with fuzz and fine agglutinated dust.

A pale, watery green sea of Mason jars, and a pile of rubbish onions that had sprouted sickly lianas curling over each other and then withered to crumble are in a dark corner and near them is a croakersack of peanuts, slashed open by some hunger and spilled out like doubloons and now only shriveled husks. And there is a crock, cold to feel, and marbeled like an aged agate.

There stands a churn that has not turned for years.

And behold a group of dolls, limp and dignified, like ancestors sitting together; and some blueing bottles filled with gentian light; and a small tarnished silver key. Away in the farthest end of the loft a big rusted tusk of a plow curves out of the shadow.

The loot of the loft lies like treasure in some thief's lair, and the thief is everywhere so powerfully present I can feel him gathering and fumbling and destroying. Yet all is so silent, except for a tinkling and occasional shiftings like the sound of a page turned in a book.

And then I find the two chests that belonged to you. On the outside is printed GAYETY SHOWS AND COMPANY. Inside I find out your whole secret.

Inside is a corroded violin whose bow has molded strings furred with raveling, like a rat of hair; some peeling gilded tap-shoes whose taps are thin from much dancing. And false faces, with tragic-gay bent down eyes, women's wigs, tubes of make-up grease, and spangles spilled over the clothes like dried fishscales. And there are fringed gypsy shawls, and scarves, crimson and jacinth and one green as a ragged peacock. I touch a scarf and it falls into air and light and seems to evanesce. And there is a yellow glove and here is a mandarin's lavish emerald-mauve gown with sleeves hanging like pointed asses' ears, with intricate work of golden braid laid tarnished over the hem.

And here is a crushed paper bird on a stick.

Sifted all among the treasures of the chests are letters and photographs of many beautiful played-out people, like lost cards, dealt and used for win or loss and cast away.

At the end of the loft room is an old dresser with a swung mirror. I go there. On the dresser is a pincushion made like a tomato, a mending box full of buttons, a cameo box of beads and cameos and bracelets and balls of faded yarn. Spiders and dust have claimed them all. Next to the dresser is an old ruptured and gutted chair.

"I give you this glass," your voice whispers, "in which to see a vision of yourself, for this is why you've come. My breath is on the glass and you must wipe away my breath to see your own image."

In the mirror I cannot see myself but only an image of dust. I brush it off—and then see my portrait there. For a moment I look like Folner! Within that cornered face, in the purple hollows and fosses of its umbrageous landscape, lie agonies like bruises; this face is thus bruised unreal. But age and time have blown their rheumy breath on the mirror and curdled it and it clouds again. Then I blow my own breath upon the mirror and wipe it clear for another instant. I seem old, I seem unused, as these loft things, in the capture of some thief. The mirror seems to say, "Dance! Swagger with a cane and sequins!"

I cry out, "Folner!" in the loft. But only the rustle of startled creatures and the faint swinging of webs respond.

(I think he ate some kind of bitterweed and suffered a

change for the eating and sprang away into a marvelous haunted and haunting world and never could return— although they waited in Charity for him—nor wanted to. Until he was washed (as I am washed against this wall) dead—like uprooted coral weed by some violence only the sea knows and only the sea-depths suffer, upon the oil-rimed and sawdusted shingle of Charity—and was claimed and buried there. They were all looking for him, waiting and watching, and looking for some grass that might take them to him—Granny Ganchion, Berryben, Malley Ganchion, Aunty, Sue Emma—and even I. And I, having not waited but wandered for him (calling, "Draw me; I will follow!" but he murmured, "Whither I go you may not follow me."), have come back here where I think I might find the magic he found among the bitterweeds and ate that liberated him and so myself be liberated into understanding and cruel authenticity.

"Love in the cotton gin, my dear. And once, very early in the delicate watergreen shell of morning, in an old moored shellbarge on Green's Bayou down around the Battlegrounds. We got tar on us.

"The C.C.C. Camp at Groveton didn't help. Ah the East Texas woods in the fall, with flying red leaves like desires, and the smell of burning brush and that dangerous, voluptuous wind of a norther that stabbed the heart, so evil; like Spanish Fly on the soul . . . Do I shock you? Of course I say these things, which are absolutely true, to shock you, you are so good, Boy, you and Berryben are so damned sweet and good, such damned sweet kids."

And you dazzled your opal cufflinks at your white wrists.

"Something cursed me. There was that melancholy always over me, brooding over me. Why? As far back as I can remember, lying on the pallet in the summer of the afternoons, there was the drone of the electric fan, like the drone of bees, and Mama going through the rooms in her slip. I felt frail and limp. It was just sorrow bred in me, bred in you too, you'll see; we are the sons of grief at cricket. I had to stop it.

"I was wild for the world of a flashing eye and life castanetting round and stomping an insinuating foot. Sometimes in Charity I couldn't stand it any longer and would go out in the henhouse and make up dreams and play like I was something grand and royal and march up and down with a poker for a cane, with only the chickens to watch me. And then love myself and feel *real* again, a kind of tremor from the world ran through me.

"Behold my talents: Started out in the Church with good Hattie Clegg, led Young People's programs, gave the main speech, sang a solo, then a duet with some girl, then said the final Benediction—it was all my show. Went to Conferences at Lon Morris College, even signed up to be a missionary. I was just looking for some passionate cause in the world to give myself to (so are all of you, all of you)—can I help it if the Church petered out for me? Then I turned to music and the stage. At the high school I was in every play that was put on and I even wrote an original musical show for the Senior Night; and at Grace Methodist Church I was always directing plays, sang in the choir, sang solos, did impersonations on programs in Fellowship Hall, played the piano by ear, anything that was make-believe. To make me forget that cisternwheel turning and turning and that old shuttered house and the family Sundays on the front porch.

"O the drone of the flies and the bees droning in the zinnias like a sound blown by a child on a comb and a piece of tissue-paper; and the melancholy working of the wind in the trees and a whole dead town gleaming out before us in a false serenity under the burning sun of a fleecy summer Sunday sky with a piece of a moon in it, and nothing happening.

"When the circus came to Bailey's Pasture, I knew this was my chance. Remember how you and I and Aunt Malley went and what we saw and did, the yellow-skinned grinning freaks in their stalls with the sawdust floor, twisted like worms the freaks grinned and ground in the sawdust; and the screams of the animals in the menagerie and the sad, exciting music of the calliope? I bought you a paper bird on a stick and here it is, crushed in this loft, to try to tell you something, to try to tell you, even then, that you were lost in Charity and that you had to get away, like me, chiming Charity Cock, to turn in the wind towards the wind's four corners, steeple-cock, welded to Charity churchtops, chanting in the wind. Remember when I lifted you up on that big elephant, you little scared thing perched on that enormous back, you shook and cried and got so excited you almost fainted and Aunt Malley had to run to buy some lemonade and throw it in your face. We were going through the world in Bailey's Pasture that night, my own world, and I wanted to tell you then that I would never see you again and that the world was like this circus, stall by stall and dazzling Fairies Wheel, and lights and tights, whirling and gleaming and screaming and twisting on a sawdust floor. We stood and watched the birdman clawing his scaly horned hands into the sawdust. Then I took you and Malley home and slipped away again, back to the circus; and met a trapeze man with thighs in black tights; and stayed and went away with the circus early that next morning. As we rolled away in our gay wagons, the last thing I saw of the house where you lay sleeping was the wheel turning over it, and the only one in that whole house that I cried for was you, Boy O Boy.

"In San Antonio I left the circus and took tap dancing at Hallie Beth Stevens' Studio of the Dance, sang out in front of a chorus of tapping girls, had a cane and a hat, and strutted singing, 'You've Got Me in the Palm of Your Hand'—not before chickens in a Charity henhouse but a real clapping audience.

"The rest I needn't tell you. Bailey's Pasture was my revelation.

"They treated me as though I was a freak in Charity, and I know it was just jealousy and envy. They blamed it on my mother, your Granny Ganchion, because she dressed me like a girl when I was little and called me 'Follie.' But it was more than that. Right away I learned what I was and went on like that, what I was and *used* myself for that, made no bones about—and can't say the same for most of the rest of Charity who don't know *who* they are. What matters if it got me death?

"But if you're going to start calling names, I can tell you a few things about Brother Ramsey in the church, who knew me all my life and even preached my funeral sermon, and who taught me a lot of what I know. Everything in this world is not black and white, as little Charity thinks; there are shades in between. And I can tell some dirt on Jim Lucas and Mimi Day Calkins—sitting there in the Pastime Club with her finger in his fly—and Floydell Lucas, his wife, bent over a cradle at home singing a lullaby—and a lot of other things. (We are all broken over the cradle, Boy.) Nobody's hands are clean in Charity. But let Charity flick its old toad's tongue after the gay green and golden summer flies—and let them croak away that same old croaking tune. They don't want anybody to be anything that they can't understand and give a name to. They had to have some ready label to lick and stick on you; and when they couldn't figure me out because I wanted different things from what they in Charity wanted, they started bullying me and torturing me. They were all really afraid of me—and most of them envied me, really envied me.

"The whine and shriek of the planing mill was always in my head, as though they were dressing ship-lap in my brain. And that hard little mouth of hunger pressing hot against my soul. To be fed! Who could feed it in Charity? Oh Charity, I would thou wert cold or hot, but because thou art lukewarm I will spew thee out!

"I take along some memories. The sight of the black watertower squatting like a fat-bellied reptile over Charity eggs; and the old house smelling of O-Cedar Oil; that old yard of guineas and cackling hens and the manure of cows. But Boy, we had a time of it, didn't we? You little frightened thing, always frightened. On one Easter Sunday I taught you a secret. We rolled away some stone, remember?"

"And you don't know how hard I prayed in the barn in the sunsets I thought were the burning end of the world, Follie. You made me feel so full of sin that I never mentioned your name to anybody; and when once and a while they would say your name I would tremble and think they knew. When the Riverbottom Nigras came to town to tell that they had seen a Haint walking in the sloughs of the riverbottoms I knew it was you come back and at night I lay

and watched, trembling on the wall, the shadow of the paper
bird made by the firelight, and I thought I heard its
annunciation: *Come away*; and I had nightmares of a haunted
bird at night, and never left the kitchen all day, sitting
trembling by the woodstove. I thought I heard you at the
windows, scratching; and once I am sure I saw you sitting in
the Beantree with the three black hens that lived up there.
When the preacher spoke about Sin it always had your face. I
have just found your real face, Follie my Follie."

"Oh Boy, I had to have some drama in a life. I had a
rhapsody in me. But it devoured me. I was so afraid of what I
found out that I began to run and run from it until I melted
down into this death. Can you learn anything from this? Tell
it—for me; someone has to tell it.

"Somewhere beyond all this muck and dreck there lies a
pasture of serenity and I will find it. I am on my way. Hang a
wreath on the door of this fallen house for me. How did I
die? I invited Death. Because I was so very weary. The rest is
a secret never to be told (see seven crows). Leave us alone
and we will destroy ourselves in the end, but we will leave
undestroyed our other selves to breathe the bridges of breath
between our ruined and isolate islands.

"I am the Ur-Follie of many derivations of your time.
Find me on walls, most prophetically adumbrated; in
shadows of firelight; bursting from clocks; turning on
steeples. And I am the beast-muzzled Prince, blacklipped and
riverlapping, begging the miracle. Give, and change the Beast.
Watch."

"I watch and watch and watch, Follie, and I will build a
bridge between these ruined islands; then blow the bridge of

breath away. But the islands will remain forever like stone islands in a still and frozen sea. For we are only breath to blow and bridge eternal ruins while we breathe, until we are blown away."

*from In a Farther Country*

# The Road Runner In Woolworth's

TWO blocks west on West Twenty-third Street was an enormous Woolworth's, and it was there that Marietta McGee-Chavez began to visit every day. To those who saw her there, she was just one of those ladies in large cities who seem to be living somewhere else . . . where could it be?

She would loiter in a corner of Woolworth's knocked about by passing crowds as she dispassionately munched her hotdog or her ice-cream sandwich. She was at home where there were so many bright objects she could mull through and occasionally buy and where there was a passage of strangers. Where was her other home? Woolworth's might have asked itself.

Her dress was old and of another time; which time was it? It seemed ageless, clean, foreign: a whitish blouse with a red embroidered figure of a bullfighter in a daring gesture across her breast, and flower petals that could be a poinsettia's clustered around the throat where the blouse was drawn like the mouth of a loose sack by a silver cord resembling a shoelace. There was a string of large clear beads around her neck such as country grandmothers once wore. Her skirt was dyed black; it must once have had red blossom shapes on it for they had burnt through a little. Her shoes seemed sad, like the string of beads. They seemed an attempt to bring down to earth in their plainness what wanted to be flighty in that territory between them and the plain beads. The shoes were old-fashioned laced-up ones and were shoes for walking upon ground.

In time she would loosen the mouth of her handmade handbag, embroidered of gold and silver threads upon a field of some blue stuff and which she carried strung around her right wrist, and pull out of it, after fumbling, a plastic heart-shaped box with *Sweetheart* written on it. People of Woolworth's knew that she had bought it there. Inside the plastic box was her watch, nestled in a bed of cotton, which she could not for some reason wear round her wrist—one of her secret problems which she had so solved for herself. She felt, probably, that it would infect her skin; or she wished to preserve the watch out of some secret sentiment for it. She would take the plastic box out of her handbag and look at the time, then put it back, munching her sandwich. What had she to do with her time?

She wore a scarf around her left wrist, caught in an oriental-looking bracelet of heavy chain and from which there dangled a large dollar-shaped medallion of a Buddha in filigree. The scarf had the names of the capitals of the world printed in large letters on it, and it was scented with toilet water from these counters.

There she stood in Woolworth's, placid and at her ease, at noon on an autumn day. Her neck was rough and her skin was papery and folded; where it folded it had cracked; in one of the cracks that curved from the flange of her nose to the corner of her mouth was a large brown mole. Her teeth were white and large, but her lips were so scarce and precarious that they had barely got onto her face, and then not quite in the proper place, causing a startling relationship between the other facial components: enormous aghast eyes as if their responsibility were to hold themselves wide and motionlessly open in a bracing starè and so brace back, like firm boulders, an impending castastrophe of hair lodged above them on too small a foundation. She was tall and rather terrible looking at first few glances because of her fowl-like profile; Spanish, perhaps—but some race modified by the influences of a large hybridizing city and some little far-off buried town in America. She had a great classic nose, a kind of gobbler's loose and manifold throat and the most insignificant little chin, merely a crease. Her face was long and narrow and above it was her uncertain small head where she piled her abundant woven and dyed black hair on top—literally a mounting for the many small Spanish combs she had set in there and a few plastic Woolworth flowerlets added. The rest of her was very long and rather endless beneath the long skirt she wore, for she descended down her person somewhere under the skirt to these sad plain feet not large enough to keep a bird balanced. This gave her a toppling gait as she walked away so that she seemed to be of the most precious frailty. Yes, she is surely some part Spanish, or has Spanish illusions, Woolworth's decided.

But what lived in this human artifice? It was as though two opposing ideas had pieced her together and the rival parts still struggled with each other upon her person. What had brought her to this shape. What dream did it hold, what flourished fancy gone to seed?

She adored the odors and objects of the world inside this Woolworth's. She was here every day to smell and touch it. If one worked in Woolworth's and watched for her, he would see her arrive, precisely at noon, maunder through the glass door on West Twenty-third Street, stand for a moment and look the whole confusion over as if she were saying to

herself, "Hello again, Woolworth's; well, now, let's see . . ."
She seemed unhurried, unenthusiastic. She asked the same
question every day, "Where is the lunch counter?" as though
Woolworth's were a vast uncharted country where one could
never find his way alone; it seemed endlessly changing and
explorable; the counters shifted their very objects overnight,
as if some mischievous floorwalker shook the store like a
kaleidoscope every night. Her pleasure was plastics: curtains,
tablecloths, dishes, spoons, flowers and ornaments; she had
touched them every one. They seemed constantly changing
their frontier. She would have to ask where they were again.
Then the floorwalker, ready for the same daily question,
would spot her standing suddenly confused in a corner, and
go over to tell her where they were, just where they had
always been. She would give the floorwalker her same thanks
and amble on there.

But most of the time she was silent and inexpressive,
just a curious nameless transient passing through, day after
day like all the others. She felt she never saw the same people
twice in there, only the employees were permanent, changing
the landscape of this country of little marvels every day; the
rest was a numberless wandering throng moving up and down
the long aisles of paths bordered by flower beds of counters
of nylon and plastic, lotion and powder and paste, lighted by
fluorescent neon, passing in and out through the swinging
glass door, on and on, where had they come from, what had
they done or seen, where were they going, what were they
looking for, to buy.

Though she was apparently shy and buried within
herself, she was quite in control of herself; for one rare time
when she interrupted the clerk in the pet department to
advise a customer of some abominable habit of canaries—she

did not seem to favor this bird—the clerk was annoyed and turned to her, whom he knew well, and said, "Listen lady, who works here?"

"Why, you do," she answered tenderly in that cool purplish tone of her voice, and showed such a gentle face that who could be annoyed with her for long?

Where had she come from and what life had she known, somewhere before? Woolworth's might have wondered. Had she been pushed back into this colossal city from some faraway forgotten wilderness? What could she tell to Woolworth's?

A memory of Marietta's, one of home, was Kresses that she adored in a nearby town of Lubbock, Texas, where she went some summers to stay with her aunt. In that hot, sultry wonderplace in the summer, there would be the boys loitering around the counters, the pretty salesgirls just graduated from high school and whom she wished she looked like, with long curls and sweetheart faces; or the mean flapper with the little pink harelip, not caring about anything in her blood-red lipstick and hoop earrings, and singing some torchsong as she arranged the boxes and bottles and tubes on her counter; someone calling, "Number six please! number six!.. and holding in the air a five-dollar bill to be changed if ever number six would come with the money bag; and over it all, in the sky of Kresses, was the busy trolley clicking and carrying the money tubes up to the cloudy balcony where three pep-girls sat aloft emptying and filling them and knocking and rolling them around while they seemed to be confiding things in each other that might be about the whole dream of Kresses they were causing to happen below. It was a place of sounds and smells and milling people, with the

Negroes wandering and gazing and handling, rubbing past you with their spongy hips, buying ruby jewelry or peanut brittle or red rubber sponges or hair pomade and adding their smell to the smell of toilet water and talcum powder and bath soap which the ceiling fans, groaning in their lazy constellations above, fanned over the place and mixed all together in their wind to make a Kresses smell. Then there was the record department where a record was always playing; and at the sheet-music counter a happy, tempestuous woman tossing on the swivel piano stool and with a head of water hair set in stormy waves, confused the phonograph music by playing any song a customer requested to hear, in her pitching style, or any she chose to play when there were no customers, to try to get some. She sometimes even sang the song she played, but in the plainest voice, and if it was sad she calmed all over, and it seemed to be about something that had happened to her; or if she did not personally care for it, she gazed out over the store thinking about something else, and tossed on. Then, though, there were no nylons or plastics, no pet department, no pinkish fluorescent lights like this New York Woolworth's that Marietta McGee-Chavez adored and took for her very own again. The smells had changed—who knew for better or worse—the objects had changed, the whole world had changed since that old Kresses in Lubbock that had been her only alternation to the fields of the faraway valley where she lived in New Mexico. But there was the same old enchantment here, something of the whole world in it, and with the pet department added—and now with this familiar bird suddenly there, faded and languishing, living for sale in the pet department of Woolworth's.

This bird had been bought off a ship from Brazil, retail, with a load of canaries, the clerk in the pet department said, and was a faded-out macaw. But Marietta knew that he was very much like the road runner she had known in her native country, called there, among her people, *"correr del paisano,"* which meant "a messenger of his countrymen," the people said. But his common name was road runner. The road runner, a good wild plain bird, could be seen running up and down the roads of the valley, shy and alone and ugly but red and golden breasted, magnificent in that part of him, and perking up a knotty little head with goggle-eyes in it, a plucked-looking and ragged long tail at the end of him, and running on strong foolish slew-feet. He could run all the long roads of the world, he was so strong and tireless.

He was a strange combination of wildness and awkwardness, beauty and plainness, a frivolous, sad and wise creature adored by all and considered sacred and of good word and omen by the people of that country. When the Highway was built through the valley, the people saw on the asphalt the scattered feathers of the road runner's lovely breast and often the crushed corpses of a whole massacred bird. Many gathered and saved the feathers of the dead bird's breast as they had saved those shed by the live birds in the fields or on the old dirt roads: stuffed in a pillow, they would cause a sweet dream and bring a peaceful death. Some road runners had withdrawn into the chaparral hills, though not many were left anywhere, any more. Marietta McGee-Chavez' father had considered the massacre of the road runner an evil turn of the world and said it was the end of an old time and the beginning of a sad new one, and that a message to the world was destroyed in him, as if a letter or a will had been torn up in the wind and blown over the countryside.

Once she had found the ragged bird in the pet department, Marietta went every day to Woolworth's to see just him. She would march straight to the back of the store, no longer looking or giving her time to anything on the counters or running her fingers over the nylon scarves and the plastic flowers as she passed them. And standing before the bird she would gaze silently at him and eat her sandwich—but the clerk would not allow her to feed the bird any of it. She would stand watching the bird, looking at his faded breast, until they closed the store and told her she was the last one in it and to leave. Marietta and the bird got to know each other and every day he would wait for her to come. Then she would stand and look at him and turn to the clerk to say, "How is the old fellow today?"

"Tired," the clerk would answer. "He will not live much longer, for he is very old and sick of Woolworth's. He dies for want of his native country."

"Has he been reduced in price," Marietta McGee-Chavez would ask, "since his longevity is so reduced?"

"No, lady," the clerk would say. "The old macaw is still twenty-four fifty, because he is a rare bird and not often seen in these parts, bought off a ship from Rio with a bunch of canaries."

"He is not in the least a macaw but a simple road runner that I know well," Marietta would preach to the clerk, "and his price is exorbitant."

"Road runner or not," the clerk said, "he has been classified as a macaw and must sell for that, and at a macaw's price, which is twenty-four fifty—prices on everything have gone up."

"He ought to be presented to the zoo, then," she told the clerk. "For he is a bird with an old history. He has a past and ought to be put on record in a zoo for historical interest."

"You tell that to Woolworth's," the clerk replied.

At night, when she had to leave Woolworth's because she was the last person in it and they were closing, she would come home and sit in her room and worry about the bird, how he was all night long and whether he was dying in the cold Woolworth's night, a sad enough place for a road runner to be even in the daytime, where there were no roads. Her pay at the "Artifices of Spain" was not much and the cost of life in New York City took more and more of it, leaving nothing to spend on a dying bird. Still, she saved back what she could each week, bought no more plastics, hoping what she could save would amount up to twenty-four fifty before the bird perished. Then he could have a pleasant, loving and native place to die in—or he might, restored to his country, which was the very same as hers, live on a little and call his call again, for her to hear. And if he died, then she would make sure his grave, wherever she had to go to find it.

She loved the bird all over and gazed at every feather of him when she was before him; but at home at night it was the breast of the bird that lingered with her, for here was where a passionate dream of a field lay faded and perishing. Though it was surely dying and its luster of feather gone, the bosom of this exiled creature kept all its lost country.

She began to roam the vicinity of the closed Woolworth's at night, to be near the bird. No one seemed to notice her when she loitered at the locked glass doors on West Twenty-third Street. In that neighborhood you could do almost anything and in plain view of passersby and no one would notice, or if he noticed he would not care but pass on. One night she saw a dim light on in the back of Woolworth's, and she peered through the glass wall that separated her from the bird's lonely world inside. There she saw the figure of the pet department clerk moving about in the shadows. She knocked on the glass door. Happily the gigantic moving vans had not begun to travel across Twenty-third Street yet and there was not too much street noise. The clerk heard the knocking and she saw him coming toward the glass door like a ghost in the aisle where all the counters were covered with black cloth. He recognized her and motioned to her to go away. She kept knocking and motioned to him to let her in. She knocked louder and louder until the clerk gave her a sign to come around to the supply entrance on West Twenty-fourth Street. Marietta ran quickly around.

At the supply entrance on West Twenty-fourth Street, the clerk was waiting for her at the door, hushing her and making a sign that Woolworth's was closed.

"But I would like to inquire if the old road runner has taken a turn for the worse that has brought you here in the middle of the night to sit up with him," she whispered.

"He is all right, lady," the clerk said. "And I do not wish to have to report you to the police patrol that will patrol by here shortly. So I advise you go to away."

Marietta reached into her purse and drew out the plastic heart-shaped box with her watch in it. "It is only nine o'clock," she advised him. "The hour my father died with this watch in his pocket, and it is an heirloom."

"It is ten o'clock, lady," the clerk whispered; and now he was nervous and exasperated. "If you are going to have a conversation come in here and let me close the door or we will both be in some trouble with Woolworth's."

Marietta quickly slipped inside the store. Inside Woolworth's, with the door locked, the clerk seemed nicer. Yet Woolworth's was a very different place indeed, even as the clerk. He had even a different look in his face. Now he was very kind, and said in a soft voice, "Would you like to come on over to the pet department and have you a seat? We can talk a little if we whisper. This is against the rules and could cost me my job, which I am very willing to lose except for the sake of the pets."

They walked to the pet department which was a shadowy place in the deepest bosom of Woolworth's, lit by the dim light of the adjacent supply room. "You have a nice little place here," Marietta McGee-Chavez said to the clerk. "But where," she asked, looking around, "is Woolworth's?"

"All covered up," the clerk said.

"It isn't the same at night," Marietta whispered.

"It's a good place to come at night, and quieter than most," the clerk said. "And I am telling you a secret which you must never divulge, for it would get me and the pets into very serious trouble with Woolworth's. I don't do any harm to anything, only come and sit with the pets, to give them some company and myself some too. They have a bad life and I do as much as I can to make it better for them. I worry about them a lot. I worry about humanity a lot, too. My room on Hudson Street is noisy with people fighting each other in their apartments and TV sets turned on so loud you can scarcely hear the trucks that begin to travel Hudson Street around eleven o'clock at night. There is so much fighting and dissatisfaction in the world, lady," the clerk said in his whisper and looking away over the dark landscape of Woolworth's; "and many people thought the advent of television would help, but it hasn't changed anything, so far as I can tell."

"Nobody knows what they want to do with each other or with anything," Marietta said.

"Sit down," the clerk whispered.

Marietta sat down in the little square that was the pet department in the daytime. All the pets were covered with their black night cozies, and occasionally there was a faint scissors-sound from the cages of the birds.

"How are they all?" Marietta asked.

"Trying to get some sleep before the trucks on Twenty-third Street begin," the clerk said. "Even the goldfish are sleeping."

"I never cared for them, asleep or awake," Marietta said. "But I smell some pine trees, to my soul."

"That is Pine o'Pine, which I spray the pet department with at night to keep the odors of the cosmetics counters out," the clerk told her. "The pets can't stand Woolworth's odors day and night."

"I couldn't either," Marietta answered.

Suddenly Marietta whispered, "What is that walking way over there in the aisle by what is from time to time the buttons counter?" A figure was moving in long strides along a distant dark aisle.

"That is just the floorwalker," the clerk said, "and another secret you must never tell, or more trouble will ensue. She comes here many nights, to walk and find some peace, I guess, and to think. I don't know. I let her alone and she lets me alone. Once in a while we talk when she walks over to smoke a cigarette and visit me here in the pet department; but generally she goes on walking up and down the aisles. She doesn't harm anything."

"But I believe she is coming this way now," Marietta whispered.

"To pay me a short visit, no doubt," the clerk said. "But she won't stay long, as she has a slight sneezing reaction to Pine o'Pine."

Sure enough, the floorwalker was coming. She came solidly, evenly, in her loping floorwalk, and Marietta and the clerk watched her slowly emerge from the darkness into the dim light of the pet department.

"Hello, Louisa," the clerk greeted her in a whisper. "Won't you stop by for a minute?"

The floorwalker stood still, looking enormous, and stared at Marietta. She was a large swearing woman with a mannish haircut and wearing men's hiking trousers. Watching her walk, one felt she could travel on endlessly without faltering, on and on. The floorwalker was going to be tough at first and sneezed and then said, in a tough whisper, "Eddie, I think this intruder should be bounced from the store, which is closed."

"She has to act as a bouncer from Woolworth's sometimes, too, besides her duties as a floorwalker," Eddie informed Marietta. And to the floorwalker he said, "She's doing no harm and she has promised to keep this all a secret. I trust this lady, who I know well by face, and you do, too, if you will look closely."

"I know her well by face," the floorwalker said, "but I am not sure I trust her." Then she pulled out a cigarette from her pocket and lit it, puffed and blew the smoke into the light of the pet department, and added, "But who do I trust?"

"You are asking yourself," Marietta said to her.

"You shouldn't have struck that match in here, Louisa," Eddie warned her.

"If I'm asking myself I'll answer myself," Louisa said. "Nobody, not any farther than I could flick this cigarette butt."

"You enjoy walking, don't you, Louisa," Marietta said.

"Sure," Louisa answered. "It's good for the brains." She sneezed.

"Where all do you go when you walk at night?" asked Marietta.

"Everywhere but past the incense counter," Louisa said through an enormous mouth that boiled out cigarette smoke.

"She's allergic to incense," Eddie said, "which is unfortunate and a devilish trick of the manager who knows that Ida is Louisa's best friend in Woolworth's or anywhere, yet he assigned Ida to the incense counter."

"The manager is a little shrimp," Louisa said, "but I can manage him. What happened yesterday was that when the manager found Ida, with a lot of time on her hands—who the hell buys incense; there are no customers much for incense— and a victim of the time-killing habit of biting her fingernails down to her capillaries, had intelligently developed the habit of drawing faces on her fingernails with a fountain pen to break the biting habit, he was going to fire her completely out of Woolworth's, until I convinced him that he ought to move her to the toy counter where she would have to wind up a loud crickety-sounding dancing Sambo all day long to keep her hands occupied. The manager put that little silver-headed doll named Margrette—that's the spelling on her time card, pure show-off spelling—on incense. Ida and I had a knock-down drag-out tonight because she says she'll lose her mind winding the dancing Sambo all day and blames it all on me. What can you do? You form one habit to break another, we are all creatures of habit, so what the hell can you do with anything, anybody? That's why I decided to take a walk tonight, to just think about how we are all nothing but creatures of habit." She ground her burnt-out cigarette on the floor.

"Please be careful and don't start a fire," Eddie told her.

Louisa was turning to do some more walking, but she stopped and looked back at Marietta to tell her one more thing.

"Do you realize lady," she said, "that in all the walking I have done in Woolworth's I could have got clear to Arizona by this time and breathed me some fresh air instead of talcum powder and hair oil with Lanolin and toothpaste with chlorophyll and fifty other things with something added? The world is taking a terrible turn, if you think about it—something is being added to everything. It will suddenly stop when somebody revolutionizes the industry by deciding to take everything out of something except what is there to start with. Then we will just have the simple thing again. For a little while we will have very brief labels; and then somebody will have to add something again. In and out, that's the story of the world."

"When I was young," Marietta said, "we didn't have all that. You have so many problems to think about as you walk."

"I would like to remind you of the problems I walk through all day long," the floorwalker said. "For instance, the cold-cream woman giving her demonstrations with her face larded in vanishing cream and who thinks she is the Million Dollar Baby in here. To try to keep her from smoking during a demonstration takes more time than I've got. She'll sneak a cigarette through that greasy hole of a mouth if I turn my back on her one second. So I have to keep a constant lookout on her. This of course gives the shoplifters a good chance. . . . Though her cigarette vanishes, when there are ashes in the cold cream, that's how I can tell. But all this takes time."

"Oh, I recognize your walking problems, Louisa," Marietta sympathized with her. "But as my job is sedentary, I have to sit through just as many."

"The world is so full of problems," Eddie said. The floorwalker turned and walked on away, down some endless-looking aisle and into the farther darkness of Woolworth's.

"She and Ida are saving up enough money to buy them a trailer house and get out of Woolworth's and travel west, just living on the highway," Eddie said. "But one more thing you must promise to tell no one in the world," Eddie continued, "is that I found on Forty-second Street a phonograph record of some birdcalls, and I have learned them by heart. It has proved an interesting thing to me, and that is that what is written on the record to be the call of the finch turns out to be, in actual practice here in Woolworth's, the woodcock's. The finch, one of our best-sellers, will absolutely not call it to me. As Woolworth's has no woodcocks for sale, that pretty call is lost. I have thereby discovered an important discovery: that the birds here are all mixed up or misnamed."

"Wouldn't you be?" asked Marietta. "Which is what I have told you about the what you call 'macaw.' Your 'macaw' is a road runner."

"The macaw is a heartless imitator," Eddie pronounced. "So where are we?"

"In Woolworth's," Marietta McGee-Chavez answered him firmly, "and it is a road runner."

"Nevertheless," Eddie said, "about the phonograph of birdcalls. I whistle them softly in here at night, while the floorwalker walks, so that the birds can have some notion of the woods they came from; and sitting in their darkness behind the night cloths, all the people gone and no longer staring at them all day long, they can think they are among their kind and home again. I have to do it before the trucks start, or they could never hear me or I them. You ought to hear them all, sometimes. It's like a wildwood in here when I get them all to answering. Not very pleasant for the goldfish, who want to sleep; but then it is my firm belief, after living years with goldfish, that goldfish do not have any hearing."

"You are doing a noteworthy thing," Marietta said, "and one Woolworth's should thank you for, if they only knew. But, tell me, does the road runner ever make his call?"

Eddie grew very said looking and said quietly, "Sometimes at night I let him out to stand up, just to stretch—his cage is too small for such a lanky bird, but then Woolworth's was not prepared for him—and then what he suddenly does, once in a great while, is to run and call for a moment, as if he had found some road taking him where he dreams to go while he sits in the cage all day. Then I do not chase him but I sit and listen to his horned feet scratching the cement floor of Woolworth's and hear him call way off somewhere, and almost want to follow him. Usually the floorwalker catches him and brings him back, and he is very exhausted from his journey."

"That is why I sometimes saw on the plastics counter or once and a while on the floor or in some corner of Woolworth's in the daytime what I thought was a little feather of a road runner and thought it just my imagination," Marietta said.

"That could be," Eddie said, "for he is shedding a lot right now; though I hope not or it would be circumstantial evidence against me and cause serious run-ins with the manager."

"Could I hold the road runner for a minute?" Marietta

asked Eddie. "I won't hurt him."

"It is strictly against all rules for customers to handle the stock," he said to her. "But as you have such a deepseated feeling for this macaw and, moreover, as he is surely going to die soon, I consent."

He fetched the bird from the cage and brought him to Marietta. As he handed the bird to her, soft as a pillow but with its stiffened feet hanging down as if it were lighting somewhere from the air, he said, "You may caress, for a moment, an old life ending in a sad surrounding."

Marietta took the bird and cradled him against her breast. Then she rocked the road runner to and fro, nursing a lost country. She could not say anything, but was it a tear that lay in the crevice of her cheek or was it the mole lodged there, her old family mark?

Then Eddie came to her and said, "Time's up, and too much handling weakens him."

In her lap Marietta saw some faded red and golden feathers the bird had lost there. She collected them and put them in her handbag. At home she would put them in her pillow. Then she said to Eddie, "One more thing. Could you, sir, do for me one of the birdcalls you have learned from the phonograph record?"

Eddie did not answer. He waited a moment, licked his lips and worked his mouth; and then he suddenly made a clear sound. Before he had finished there was the clearest frail answer from the dark cages. He waited a moment. Then he made another clear call. There were more answers, and in a few more moments a low burbling song began and increased and rose until all Woolworth's was softly trilling. Above the low music was the solid, even walking sound of the floorwalker's feet. But there was no sound from the old macaw.

Then Marietta stood and arched her neck and seemed so tall and thin, drawn up to a topnotch at the tip of her small head, and she whistled a wild, sad call that rose up out of her breast. In a moment there was the unsure, faraway answer. It was the old road runner.

Marietta and Eddie were very quiet. What was it the single solitary call had touched in them, in all Woolworth's, even in the floorwalker somewhere walking far away on the distant roads of aisles, as though they might have heard it before a long way back somewhere where they had been and come from and wished they could go back. The floorwalker went on walking, disappearing in the darkness of some long aisle that might have been a highway leading to a faraway desirable place where the call could have come from, passing momentarily through a faint ray of light, then vanishing again.

In this hushed moment, with only the sounds of the floorwalker's feet traveling on and on in a low solid beat, Marietta McGee-Chavez started talking in a lovely voice:

"On the far southwestern mesas, in a landscape on fire, where the sage billows like pale green puffs of smoke and the flame-shape trees lick up in the distance, was our house. My mother was a quiet country woman and tried to bring me up the same; but my father was a man with a fire Spain set in him that I worshipped. He was Spanish. He played a mandolin. He taught me the Colcha stitch, an ancient Spanish art of embroidery, and tomorrow I will come in here at noon and give you, Eddie, and the floorwalker a little embroidery that I have made, for thanks. My father told me many stories that I have not forgotten, and some I hope to tell again, sometime, as he told them, so as not to let stories be lost and never told again.

"Our landscape where we lived was lonesome; it seemed always autumn. The burning wind! Always the wind searing the broomgrass golden and whipping the flames of the cottonwood trees and churning the smoke of the sagebrush, whirling the devil-dusters over the Burnt Mesa, under a shining wide sky with only once in a while a little blue cloud shaped like a sail sailing over.

"Away across the sagebrush ran the western road to Starr's farm. The road to Starr's farm! It was a lanky dirt road starved of grass and rutted by wagon wheels and printed with hooves of horses. It went lean and dusty over a field of rock that grew in the clay where it was a glassy pass in rain or winter, past a field of horsecorn, on by a miraculous stand of unwatered Russian olives, across the wooden trough of the ditch, and then on and on through a level sea of sage. There, far at the end, under a cool grandness of enormous blowing cottonwoods, was Starr's farm. A pure stream wound through it and the cows were happy in clean grass. A large family of turkeys went their way, staying always together, over the meadow where lupines bloomed. There was an orchard of apples and pears, and the noise of many chickens. The Starrs were our only neighbors and so far away that only the distant trees, like a leafy green cloud hanging over them, marked where they lived. At twilight we heard the bawling of their cows.

"That was a long time ago. What used to be the dirt road to Starr's farm is piece of a Highway to Denver running in front of the house. It is wide and covered with asphalt. If at rare times a coyote runs red on the Highway at night, he is blinded by the headlights of a great truck—they travel by night in caravans from Albuquerque to Denver, from Denver to Albuquerque—and killed. But if a sunflower seed or the seed of broomgrass is planted in the cracks of the asphalt Highway by the wind, whole pieces of the road will be slowly overthrown by the power of some simple growing desert grass. They have to frequently repair the Highway through this country.

"Behind our house, sometimes so close you felt you could reach out and gather firewood from it, sometimes so far away it was painted on a sky of glass, was the great mountain cut, by a gorge that ran down between them, into two humps shaped like sleeping people. In the spring and early summer the melted ice from the mountain made a waterfall leap over the gorge. It was full of people shapes moving in it. On the near side of the mountain was a golden slope where there were always dark climbing figures that I saw. These were the people that I knew—and I have never seen them again. To call them back, I would have to be free and frivolous and believing again.

"Our moon, our stars! They belonged to us, to my mother and my father and me; they were as real and as ordinary as the dishes on our supper table, we could have set the table with them, they were that everyday, we had them that much in hand. The little Seven Sisters was a diamond kite flown by somebody on the mountain top; and in the autumn, at the right time, the whole moon rose exactly behind the mountain top and seemed to be a head tilted back and with open mouth blowing the kite of diamonds higher and higher, over our house where I watched it from my bed, and on beyond, over the Burnt Mesa and away on out of sight.

"In front of us stretched out the Burnt Mesa, called the *Llano Quemado* by the Spanish. It had been burned a long time ago and ever since the burning it would never grow anything again, not even grass. The people who lived there looked burnt up. All they had to sell were adobes, baked earth, the best anywhere in the valley. I saw a crazy old man there once when I went with my father to try to buy adobes and the crazy old burnt man from the *Llano Quemado* asked us if we wanted to buy his little boy who was playing in the burning sun among the baking bricks. "Why do you want to sell him?" my father asked the old Burnt Mesa man. 'Because he has never learned to speak, his tongue is burnt up by the great fire, he is no good, the old man said. 'How much is he?' I asked timidly. 'About seven dollars,' the old man told me; and he and my father laughed.

"I wanted, as my secret, to buy the little speechless boy, and I saved what I had from my allowance for a long time so that I could buy him and bring him to our house and teach him to speak and show him all the things I saw, the diamond kite, the people climbing the golden slope, the people in the waterfall. I have never told this, but when I was a year older I had saved seven dolaars. With it I ran away from our house a long way to the Burnt Mesa. I remember that a road runner ran ahead of me nearly all the way, but he would not go onto the Burnt Mesa. I came to the house of the speechless little boy and there I found the old man.

" 'I have come to buy the little boy whose tongue was burnt and cannot speak,' I said to the old man.

" 'You cannot buy him,' the old man said, 'because he is dead, buried to death under a pile of fallen dobes.' *Muerto*, he said, and the word was terrible.

"There is everything to share. If you keep things to yourself and for yourself alone, they somehow vanish—they tarnish under your own eyes and fade away, finally, from your sight. Things must be told to another, or they die. *Muerto* . . . the terrible word hung over everyting I saw and could not tell about to anyone.

"In the wintertime the snow covered the sagebrush and covered the white gleaming mountain, and in the icy air the blown white slope held its buried climbers whose breath was the blue vapor the wind blew round and round the slope. I imagined them sleeping, resting from their long climb of summer and autumn which they would have to begin again when the season changed. The waterfall was frozen and covered with snow. All my people were buried under ice.

"Over all this ran and called a devilish old bird, but with a beautiful breast. He was always with us, except in the deepest winter when he slept, warm, like the climbers of the slope, under the snow-covered chaparral tree; we knew he was there. This bird was called the road runner. The Spanish people called him the *paisano*. They said he was a messenger of his countrymen, *correr del paisano*, they called him. He was sacred and called something to the world. When he ran up and down the dirt roads or across the moors of sage and made his wild lonesome call, it was regarded as of special omen. It was said he ran calling across the Burnt Mesa before it burned, but never ran or called there again. No one would shoot him or molest him. What was he saying?

"My father told me many stories about the road runner. He surrounded sleeping rattlesnakes with prickly pears and thorns, my father told me, and when the snake awoke he found himself trapped and bit himself to death and died of his own poisoning. If you stuffed a pillow for a dying person's head with the breast feathers of a road runner, the dying person would die easy and find his road to peace—as if the road runner led him there. Another tale was that the road runner was the spirit of a cruel and stranger woman who had lived alone under the dangerous mountain and who had died saving her village from a landslide of rock off the mountain that made the gorge for the waterfall. I believe it was the woman that I saw in the waterfall. She had seen the rockslide coming and stood on her rooftop and shouted to the village to run, and in time to save the villagers, but she was buried under the falling rock. The village had not known she cared that much for them. She had owned a very beautiful bird from Spain, her native country, whose name or breed no one knew but all adored him. The bird was killed, too, in the avalanche, crying out with the woman to the village. But not long after, when the people came back to the village and dug it out of the rubble of rock, they noticed a new kind of bird among the rocks, one not ever seen before, shy and ugly and wild but with a splendid breast of feathers inherited from his ancestor; a *mestizo* they called him—as the world grows older, everything in it gets more and more mixed—is that history?—a *mestizo* because he was a mixture of absurdity and dignity, orneriness and beauty. He made them laugh because he was so comic looking and he made their hearts warm because he was so lovable and loyal and called out of some good thing ahead, even at the most despairing times when there was no crop or a whole season of dust. They depended on this old faithful messenger and could not imagine their country without him running across it. When he was driven off the land, the country perished and changed. This was hundreds of years ago, and a myth by the time I heard it from my father. You can hear many more like it if you go to that country. The bird stayed on and multiplied himself and his generations inhabited all the land of the Southwest, it is told; and this bird was the blessed and crazy old road runner."

Eddie was quiet and the floorwalker's feet were sounding on and on like the regular beat of a heart, and Marietta looked somewhere far off and said,

"What did he cry? When I used to hear that cry, it filled me with such loneliness and yet with such a message of . . . thrilling hope . . . in my breast. I would go somewhere and do something bright and good and of wide result upon the world of people who needed what I would do. His cry, a cry of daring and a cry of heartbreak, has haunted my breast all my life. I had never in my life again, after I left my country, been able to imitate the call—although I hear it many times in my breast—until just a while ago when I suddenly felt it rise up from my breast and called it." She turned to Eddie and looked straight at him.

"I want to save the bird from Woolworth's," she said. "To bring him back to something of his own, and to come back to something of my own again. You can understand this. I want to rescue and protect an old messenger and try to save an old old call that is very personal to me. In the end, what you had wanted to give the whole world, some dream for everybody, you are satisfied to have back just for yourself, to keep it that little bit true and pure, anyway—everything gets so mixed up and we lose a single way—but try as you may, it does not seem to want to come back to you; where have you lost it, what did you sell it for—it lives dumb and suffocating and trying to find its call, its message, buried in your bosom as though a mountain of rock had fallen upon it." She rested and quietened. Then she concluded:

"And that is why I ask you to sell me the old what you call macaw who, I am sure as I live and breathe and have told you this story, is not a macaw at all but simply some old misplaced and lost grieving road runner; and I have proved it to you, now. He answered my call."

The clerk was moved. He waited a moment and then said,

"The *macaw*, I am so sorry to have to tell you—though you have told a wonderful thing and I wish all Woolworth's could hear it in the daytime—is still the property of Woolworth's and is still twenty-four fifty, lady. I wish you had the cash money with which to buy him at once; and I wish I had something saved to lend you, as I have not. And I wish I made the rules here. I wish I classified the birds. The phonograph records were wrong, so maybe their names are wrong, I don't know. But finally it doesn't matter, they are all birds and make a lovely sound and you have told a beautiful thing because you imitated a call you had lost and heard it again. Couldn't you just settle for that?"

Marietta thought seriously and then said, "I will somehow find my twenty-four fifty."

The floorwalker's voice said tenderly from somewhere in the darkness, "Honey, that's all Eddie can do is to sell the bird for the price put on him. I have been walking and listening to your story and thinking how I wish I could lend you my savings I am saving to buy a Home-on-the-Road trailer-house to migrate west in; but as part of it is Ida's and as she has not heard the story, how could she ever believe what I told her; As a matter of fact," she said, walking on, "who in the world would believe it tomorrow if I told it to them here in Woolworth's when all the counters are uncovered?"

"That's the hardest part," Marietta whispered out, "to believe. If we could all only do that, just believe what we hear from each other."

"I do," Eddie said softly.

"I do," the floorwalker heard herself murmur.

"But," Eddie added, "there are rules of the store and prices and names of the articles of purchase which we all have to deal with, being employees of Woolworth's."

The floorwalker walked upon Marietta and Eddie with a look as though she had come upon a town where long ago something heartbreaking had happened to her, and said to them, "But I think we'd better all get out of here because it's time. The trucks are due to begin any minute now, and that noise would ruin the peace in Heaven, not to mention Woolworth's."

Marietta took out her plastic heart-shaped box from her embroidered handbag and saw that it was nine o'clock.

"It *is* nine o'clock," she said.

And suddenly the distant rumble caused Woolworth's to tremble a little—the trucks were coming.

"Good night," they all said; and they crept out the supply entrance and went their different ways, as they saw, coming towards them from the Hudson River, the lighted caravan of trucks grinding up the empty aisle of Twenty-third Street.

Marietta McGee-Chavez went to her room above the "Artifices of Spain." Already it was rocking with the blasting of trucks. "I will have to prostitute the red sewing of a Flowering Thorn to Mr. MacDougal, who knows it is my masterpiece and has been bargaining for it for years and will turn around and sell it for twice what I will ask him for it. But it is for the old road runner," she resolved, "and I will do it tomorrow."

The next day Marietta went into Mr. MacDougal's workshop the first thing and announced that the Flowering

Thorn was for sale for twenty-five dollars and his to have at
once for that amount, cash money. Mr. MacDougal complained about the twenty-five dollars, then he took her hand
and pressed it and gave her that same tender suggestion which
she had seen in his eyes for the past five years and which
asked her, she very well knew, to marry him utterly and
make with him again a true, joint enterprise of "Artifices of
Spain." But he was only Irish and a dilettante of Spain, just a
Spain-teaser. She released her hand and asked him please for
the money, producing from her bosom the Flowering Thorn,
her little masterpiece, before his eyes. Mr. MacDougal
admired the sewing once again and took cash money from
the safe to give to Marietta McGee-Chavez who disappeared
quickly without other reward for him. But this was a sign of
hope for Mr. MacDougal.

She rushed at once to Woolworth's, through the
morning crowds on the sidewalk. At the glass door to the
store, she found it locked. Woolworth's had not opened yet.
There was a group of customers waiting there. She went
through them, asking, "You are not here to buy a macaw are
you?" The people seemed amused and some insulted, and no
one said he had any intention of buying a macaw that
morning. She was relieved. She would have the bird at last.
She pushed through the crowd to be the first at the door and
stood there pressed against it with her hands cupped around
her eyes to see if she could see the bird back there.

Finally the store opened and she was the first to enter,
racing to the pet department and calling out to the clerk,
whose back was turned to her,

"I have come to buy the old road runner!"

"You cannot any longer buy the old macaw, lady," the
man said, turning around to look at her darkly, "because he

is dead. Why do you think Woolworth's was late in opening this morning? The whole store is upset."

"Oh . . ." Marietta almost whispered. She was panting from running.

"I found him expired in his cage this morning," the clerk said grievously. "He could not stand the climate of the city any longer, and so he lay on his back and died last night for loss of his country."

"I cannot stand the climate of the city either, but I have not died," Marietta said to him, as if she thought that might bring the bird back to life.

"You didn't live in Woolworth's either," the man said. "The old macaw is dead."

"He died making his call," Marietta said, heartbroken.

She turned away a moment and went over to the canaries and gazed at them while she pondered—but the canaries didn't help. Then she came back to the man and said:

"How much is a dead road runner, then—to give him a good burial?"

"We could not sell a dead macaw," the man told her. And then he looked at Marietta very tenderly, a way she did not think he could ever look at another person, and said, "Don't grieve, lady; the poor old devil is better off."

Marietta turned away, and then she had to come back to the clerk once more. "Could I see him once more and for the last time?" she asked.

The clerk thought a moment and then said, "Sure, lady. Although it is strictly forbidden for customers to come in the supply room—and that is where the bird's body is—I think it could be justified to let you break the regulation on the basis that you and the old macaw were such good friends while he was alive here in Woolworth's."

"Thank you," Marietta said, and she followed the man into the supply room. There was the dead bird. She looked at his eye.

"He will not yet close his eyes," the man said, "though most dead birds do." He showed Marietta the little shutter of the bird's eyelid; and Marietta thought how when it closed a magical world would go out behind it.

"Could I ask your name?" Eddie said. Marietta handed him a card that read "Artifices of Spain," 132 West Twenty-third Street, New York City. Then she turned and walked out of Woolworth's for good and did not go to "Artifices of Spain" but walked through New York City all day long in the rain that had the smell of sagebrush in it, not knowing where to stop or what for.

At dusk she came home to the building on West Twenty-third Street, but she would not go up the fire escape to Spain and have to confront the old watchdog of Mr. MacDougal who was no doubt having his Spanish lessons and would try to get her to cue and coach him as he babbled a Dog Latin that further vulgarized such a pure romance language.

She went into "Artifices of Spain," locked the barrier to it and sat down in the back of the shop under one light. As soon as she had settled she could already hear Mr. MacDougal upstairs in the living room on the border of Spain, as if he were camping there waiting for some passport to smuggle himself in with, listening to his phonograph record speaking Spanish for him to learn: *yo q-u-i-e-r-o:* "I wish"; *tu q-u-i-e-r-e-s:* "thou wishest"; *Usted q-u-i-e-r-e;* "you wish." And then the little intermezzo of Spanish music, played on a mandolin, followed, to give rest to the student and to provide a Spanish atmosphere for him. It was truly a wishing music.

Marietta McGee-Chavez sat under the light in the back of the store and thought how the breast of the bird was like a golden piece of field with frost and snow already in the far northern summits—it had winter coming to cover it—of the mountains that bordered its edge. It was a whole country. Over its eye there was a delicate little screen, so fine and so destructible that she thought a tear could tear it or a speck of sunlight pierce it and violate it. And yet it had hung, this eye, among grass, and what did it behold among the blades of grass where one drop of dew could hang like an enormous tear? And surely in the grass' tear his eye beheld, as in a mirror, a world of grass and his own eye among the grass. Had his call been for this? The greenness of his eye was like a growth of rabbitweed and the amethyst light of twilight upon it. Surely the world is grass, the bird must have thought. For look, Marietta remarked, how his feathers were like grass, manifesting the colors of all grass seasons upon them. "You blessed creature of a vast grassland," she thought, "all flesh is grass. That is the message that you cried as you ran down the road, a messenger of your countrymen."

The grass change! Surely he wore a coat of grass. Indeed, he had eaten very grass, and he was grass that the wind blew over and blossomed and withered. Surely his flesh was grass. And now he had withered.

A tear fell upon her face. She felt it slide and hang on her cheek. Was it because all flesh is grass? What caused the tear to gather and fall? she wondered, going to the window but not to look out at anything. A tear, she thought surely, holds within it, like the eye of a bird, what world made it gather and form and fall, as fruit that gathers and falls, or nuts or blossoms, hold the tree and the bush and the thorn that made and bore them and that they carry down with them when they fall. So men and women carry countries in them and, falling, the country in their breast falls in them. Surely the world is grass, Marietta thought. That was his call over the prairies and over the mesa, over sage and chemisa and broomgrass.

She sat still as though she were waiting for something; and the mandolin music played and the voice murmured, "I wish . . . thou wishest . . . you wish. . . ." Now she remembered the feathers she had gathered from the bird in Woolworth's and she stuffed them in her old pillow upon which her mother had crocheted a simple field of flowers now faded pink and yellow and blue, but on whose opposite end she had Colcha-stitched a brilliant figure of fire. She opened the new plastic zipper from Woolworth's which she had lately added to it and stuffed in the new feathers, perhaps the last she would ever gather. With what feathers she saved back in her purse, she would one day make a sewing of the road runner, to use his real feathers for the breast. She put the pillow behind her head and lay back upon it.

Then sometime in this peculiar time of stillness and what seemed like a kind of resting, there was, very certainly, a rattling of the locked barrier to "Artifices of Spain." It was a robber or a Twenty-third Street tramp. She would not answer. There was another rattling, and another. Could it be a customer? She looked up and motioned to the customer to go away. The customer motioned to her to come let him in. She went to the door in the dark to say that "Artifices of Spain" was closed and to please go away; but it was Eddie. And when she opened the barrier there stood the clerk from Woolworth's with the bird on his finger like a resurrection.

"What does this mean!" Marietta exclaimed to him.

"That the old macaw, which I had wrapped in a warm rag for a shroud in the supply room, revived himself about two p.m. this afternoon, and lo and behold he has pulled through; and that he is yours at no cost and as a present from me," the clerk said, almost singing with his surprise. "We had a dangerous crossing getting here this time of night because of all the trucks—we made it by the skin of our teeth; and he is yours. I have told Woolworth's that the macaw is dead and filled out the proper loss-of-property forms on him—for tax purposes—and no one else knows that he is as alive as ever, though naturally a little shaken from his experience, but the floorwalker, who is very happy that you have your bird; she will never tell on us."

Marietta gazed at the bird in her old tender Woolworth's way and then said, softly, "It is a miracle."

"It is a miracle, the man said, laughing with joy. "And not many miracles happen in Woolworth's; in fact none. This is a miracle and has made me see some things." He grew stern and spoke more quietly. His hand, with palm turned upwards, was against his breast; and the bird, sitting in his nestling palm, cuddled against the man's breast.

"But I must confess to you one thing," he said gravely, "and do not be heartbroken. And that is that I had taught the macaw, who will learn anything, the call which you evoked from him last night in Woolworth's. It was a call from the phonograph record. The miracle was that you suddenly called it out to him. I used an imitation to bring out from you the real call that you had forgotten. But this proves, I am afraid, that he is a macaw."

Marietta did not answer.

"But let bygones be bygones," the clerk went on. "The

point is that he is yours free of charge . . . and," the clerk said, holding out his long perch of a finger, "here is the old . . . road runner. Where the dogs can't get him."

Marietta did not know what to say, but she took the bird onto her shaking hand and they greeted each other gladly.

"One thing more," the clerk said, turning to leave. "If you do not take him away at once to his native country, he will die for good the next time."

Marietta said to the bird, "You have had a close call but for the friendship of two friends. This is a warning and a prophecy." To the man she said, "I would like to buy the old road runner, for I have the money from the sale of my Flowering Thorn."

"He is not for sale," the man said firmly.

"Then," Marietta said brightly, "I would like to make a tradelast with you, for the bird. It is something that I love and have made: and it is a tiny crown of Spain, all of silver thread and set in a clasped daguerreotype frame that once held a picture of my grandmother as a girl in Spain, and her name was Consuelo which means "I console.' It is always in my purse for luck and miracles, and now it goes to you and into your pocket as a tradelast for the road runner. It has brought me something back again and I hope it will do the same for you. And could I ask you to take this small sewing of a silver waterfall to the floorwalker as a present from me?" she said, handing it to him.

"Thank you, lady," the man said with warm gratitude, "and thank you on behalf of the floorwalker; and good luck to you and the tough old road runner." He gave the bird one quiet last look and made a soft sound in some language that was theirs, for a sad parting.

He was going out the door when he stopped to say, "You have a nice place here."

"Just an imitation," she said dryly, "but it is all right at night with all the sewing machines covered up and is a quiet place from the phonograph upstairs."

"It seems real enough to me," Eddie said. "But isn't it remarkable how the same places are different sometimes from what they really are? I think that must mean that all places are two different things that have got all mixed up together."

"You haven't seen upstairs," said Marietta. She looked at Eddie and asked, "May I ask what nationality you are?"

"Pure Irish," the clerk answered.

"You have some Spanish in you, I could vow," she said.

"Not one speck," Eddie was sorry to reply.

Then she closed the door but did not lock the gate this time, as Eddie went on away down Twenty-third Street.

*from The Fair Sister*

HIS name was Canaan Johnson and he was, I will have to admit, a smart thing. He knew Hebrew but was studying it even further. He was a teacher, black as the Ace of Spades, and asked Savata to set him up as a teacher of Hebrew to the members of the LOWHC. As we are the Black Jews by our ancestry, Savata announced to her congregation that Canaan Johnson would be at the disposal of them for $1.25 an hour as a teacher of Hebrew, which all must learn to get the true tongue of Jesus, to be rightly saved. You can't be truly saved in just translation, Canaan Johnson announced to the congregation. Naturally they were all scrambling to him with their $1.25 an hour. Before I knew it Savata had not only taken him as a boarder into her home which the church bought for her as a Bishop's Lodgings, but had appointed *him* business manager of the Light of the World Holiness Church — and I was asked to move on: to a one-and-a-half room walk-up across town.

Oh I could have hated Canaan Johnson, but I thought: first, I'll take the friendly approach to him, to get to know him and to find his loopholes. I arranged for a meeting, not at the Bishop's Lodgings (naturally), not at my walk-up, but in a neutral place: a small restaurant with a cat.

He arrived at the restaurant looking as elegant as the impresario he was. I was waiting on the bench with the cat.

We took a table.

"You are my guest, Mr. Johnson," I informed him.

"I'll have a double scotch on the rocks, little water," was his answer. I made no comment. The cat rubbed against my leg and I muttered, "keep your legs to yourself, Mr. Johnson!"

We were off to a bad start.

"Right away I can see that you are a nervous woman," remarked Canaan Johnson.

"Right away I can tell you who wouldn't be?"

"Well relax,!" he said, man-like. "I'm here for a long time."

"Well you'll pay for your own drinks, then," I told him smartly.

"Oh I don't mean *here*, Ruby Drew. I mean in the Light of the World Holiness Church."

The wretched cat jumped up on the seat beside me. I squealed and jumped like a buoy. "You just have to take this cate somewhere else," I called, embarrassed, to the waitress. "I'm too jumpy today."

"He's your friend, not mine," she called back, laughing. Canaan Johnson laughed his male laugh and I decided to laugh, too, and we were off to a better beginning. I stroked the cat.

"Now tell me where do you come from, Canaan Johnson?"

"Little Lady," he mouthed, "I sprang out of Bullfinch full-grown."

"Where's Bullfinch?"

"In Oklahoma," he snickered.

"Well I'm from Alabama," I retorted.

Canaan Johnson leaned back in his seat and made a

gesture as if he had a cloak on — grand. "I was on Theseus'
ship with the black sails, was in love with Ariadne . . ."

"I bet you was. Who's she?"

But Canaan Johnson went on. "A Princess with a crown
of stars."

"Hogwash!" I says.

"I was in the Labyrinth of the Great Bull . . ."

"That's obvious," I says. "Some of the Great Bull
rubbed off on you."

"Don't be unattractive," Canaan Johnson said.

"Well your lips are too big," I threw back at him.

"They kiss full," he said, blowing them out like
bubblegum.

"Don't be pornographic."

"All kidding aside, Ruby Drew — you are charming and
we could be friends if you'd relax and have a sense of
humour — and of history. I'm here to stay, so why don't you
relax and enjoy it? I could be a friend to you, teach you a
lot, and get you out of that trucksize rut you're in."

"We don't mesh," I says, pulling at a thread in my dress.

"It's because you don't co-operate."

"Well how can I?" I complained. "You doubletalk. I
don't know where the truth begins and the crap ends."

"Don't use such words, Miss Drew."

"Well I want to talk turkey," I says.

"Ahahahahaha!" he laughed, like a villain in the
restaurant. The cat scampered away.

"Why do you laugh? Like a goat . . ."

"An old joke comes to mind," he says.

"Well keep it to yourself."

"You're cute, you know that?" he says, with his lips
looking like a wet inner-tube.

"Oh don't be silly."

"Relax, relax!"

"Not around you."

"You're cute."

"I wish to change the subject."

"From what to what?"

"From me to you."

"All right Ruby Drew. What is it you wish to know?"

"I wish to know your background and your credentials."

"I rode with the Seven Assassins at Palumbo. We went by night on black horses."

"Who were you out go get?"

"The Wicked King."

"What'd he do?"

"Pilfered the poor . . ."

"What's that word 'pilfered' . . .?"

"Later," he made a wave of his hand. "The Wicked King ensconced himself . . ."

"Ensconced" . . . what's that? "Ensconced" . . .

"Forget it," he waved. "Don't interrupt the telling of a story by an adroit story-teller."

"Beg pardon," I said. By this time I was enthralled. Canaan Johnson went on, full-lipped, and with his words.

"The Wicked King ensconced himself in an *invisible* cave. The only way to make the cave visible was by raping the Hideous Princess, his hideous daughter."

"Don't tell dirty stories."

"This is classic, not dirty."

"Well you said rape."

"In the sense of carrying off by force. You're impossible, Ruby Drew, to tell a story to. You don't know words.

Now where the hell was I . . . and will you please shut up until I've finished."

"Granted," I says.

"As I was saying, then, the only way to make the cave of the Wicked King visible was by raping the Hideous Princess Crayfish. The Hideous Princess Crayfish was . . . unmentionably repulsive. Her hideousness was put upon her in order to keep the King's cave invisible. So — to kill the king you had to rape the Princess. On, on rode the Seven Assassins of Palumbo."

"On their black horses," I says.

"Right," answered Canaan Johnson. "On, on they rode — to the palace of the Hideous Princess Crayfish. Her palace was so vile you would not ordinarily advance within a mile of it, for it exuded sulphurous odours and was abuzz with millions upon millions of relentless gnats. There was a moat of foul water around the palace, and inside sat the Princess in a cage of barbed wire, peeling — and eating — garlic. Now how could anybody rape *that*?"

Now there was a small crowd around Canaan Johnson, listening with open mouths to his story. The cat was back and sat on its haunches, listening too.

"On, on rode the Seven Assassins of Palumbo," continued Canaan Johnson. "To our astonishment, through binoculars, about a mile from the fetid palace, we saw that it had vanished. *It* had become invisible!"

"That meant you had to rape the Wicked King in order to make the Hideous Princess visible," I says. "My God, it's too complicated. I have to go to the bathroom."

When I returned from the bathroom, I heard Canaan Johnson saying, "And that is how the Wicked King was dragged by black horses across the plains of Palumbo, by the

Seven Assassins."

"How, how?" I cried. "What happened while I was in the bathroom?"

"That's your problem, Ruby Drew," Canaan Johnson told me. "I finished the story economically while you were away. Nevertheless, I was given the greatest honour of Palumbo, a medallion with something printed on it, which I later lost in another battle. As for that episode, the Siege of Sacrosanct, I shall have to tell you of it another time. Now I have to get back to the Light of the World Holiness Church where I have pressing business."

This really hit my spine. "You have no business there!" I reproved Canaan Johnson.

"My desk is filled with papers. I must return to my work."

He rose, still as grand as if he had on a cape and sword, and I realized that I did not know one more thing about him than I knew the first day I laid eyes on him: that he was a bright crook; full of hot air; and an attractive messenger of bad news for me.

As we went out, I felt I had had to catch this thief by some other means, and so I said, "Caanan Johnson I admire your vocabulary and I would like to make you a proposition: teach me vocabulary (English) at one dollar a lesson." I was intent on getting a host of new words from him, and a story-telling ability like his, all to slay him into dumb-foundedness, his tongue cleaving to the very roof of his mouth, with my oratory. I would excell him. For *I*, too, have a natural tongue, supple to speaking, and acrobatic with words — my gift from the Lord Jesus, thanks. Canaan Johnson bit for my proposition.

"Natürlich," he said, as we left the restaurant with the

cat (where I paid the bill). "When do we begin, Little Lady?"

"Tomorrow," I stated.

"You're eager to get moving, aren't you?"

"Ruby Drew has no time to wait when she wants something," I firmly impressed him.

"Tomorrow at three," he accepted.

So we started. I decided to use my wits on him, the Lord being my ally, and thusly overthrow him, like the Prince of Darkness, with his own tools. "The cleverness of the clever I will thwart," St. Paul saith — and so saith Ruby Drew. We have to use guile for our Lord against his enemies — sometimes no matter — if 'tis for the good cause. I don't mean that I believe in going to the lengths Moniah Duke did — that is, fornicating with the fornicator. That's lust, and Moniah Duke proved it. She fell into the very coal-fire of fleshly lust and was herself converted by the convert — a terrible thing. She's now a common strumpet and can't give it up — help her Jesus. But gamble with the gambler and beat him at his own game —fire with fire. Yet don't drink with the drunkard or you're dished. I could give examples.

You see, Canaan Johnson did know his Church. He knew all the history of it, about all the old Fathers of it, and about Heretics and Schisms and all that, about the old Saints sitting up on poles in the desert, living in caves and having visions of naked temptresses; and all that. He was of a historical nature. But the Church is not history, it is the living Bread and Light. In other words, Canaan Johnson was *mental*. Mentalness never saved any soul, fed any hungry, made any light out of darkness. He was just a book walking. Mr. Bullfinch is what he was. How can a man get so smart? He sure was ruining the love of two holy sisters. But I was devising my scheme, as I have told you.

You see, the thing of Savata was that she was a woman
of learning without ever learning — the most dangerous kind.
Canaan Johnson said she was a "woman of instinct."

"You got *instinct* on the brain," I fumed at him. I
*would* not let him get the best of me. But he was a prickly
foe, as the Bible says, and had all the tools of Satan at his
use. It is obvious that there was this infernal battle between
me and Canaan Johnson, fighting over Savata's soul, caught
in-between the powers of darkness and light, with Savata the
fair prize. She was worth it — even, I think, enjoyed it. So I
told myself I would be the mental one, if Savata was the
instinct one. And I would arm myself from the very arsenal
of mine enemy and so overthrow his camp. In other words, I
would rape the King! Let him have his black horses of
Palumbo and all that invisible stuff.

Our lessons begun. Oh twas a merry chase! I wore short
dresses — to get Canaan Johnson on his instinct — and he said
I looked like a sack of potatoes with varicose veins. But I
used my mind on him and learnt good words from him. He
taught me enough verbiage to kill a Senator from the South
with. He did have a lip for the word; words just slipped forth
from those thick lips like half-sucked gum drops. I could see
that with him my mind was of more use than my instinct, as
twas the reverse with Savata.

During our lessons he tried some more long-winded
stories on me when I would try to pin him down about
certain *specifics* in his life, but I would not have them from
him. "Don't use that Bull . . . *finch* on me," I said, and got
some of his number, anyway. But I've never known a lipper
like him.

We spent a week on words from other languages. I got
*sans, natürlich, de rigueur,* etc. all straight, and pasted them

on my memory like gold stars, for they are very impressive in arguments. We also gave a full week to words of mythology: *herculean, trojan* are just a few examples; and a full week to beautiful adjectives. I got *exquisite, ravishing, impertinent,* etc. out of that.

Larded all in-between our word learning, cunningly interspersed at Canaan Johnson, were my questions of his own life and previous whereabouts. This slickster would always elude me and scamper into the bushes of terminology for cover. He ought to have been a lawyer. Or he would try that "you're cute" stuff, and attempt to play on my instinct side. But I persistently kept our relationship mental. My pore brain was glittering with words like a string of Christmas lights, and my appetite was like a hog's.

We finally had a fight to the finish over the word *epistemological,* particularly as I found his hand on my bad knee during my struggle to pronounce this fairly useless word, and so the lessons ended – in heat. "Consider me invisible," I said, "like your phony Wicked King. You'll *never* find my cave! You're a *chaise-longue* assassin!"

So I come away with my verbiage. I kept a-studying my words and learning them and memorizing them. I did synonyms and antonyms on my own and I got really sharp.

But the Canaan Johnson trouble went on – despite my vocabulary. Next thing I knew he had done disbursed 600 dollars for a piano, 3000 dollars for a pipe organ, and 100 dollars for something I could never find out.

I kept quiet (thank you Jesus) and withdrew from Savata's church. I left a quiet letter of resignation, written in some of the finest prose, and with dignity, not pride. I mailed it, registered letter. Then I put away my preaching papers and sought for myself an honourable job in house-cleaning, for an

interim living. What? No, Savata never made attempt one to
get in touch with me. I sure had to pray hard to keep
religion, I honestly tell you. With all my words in me I kept
my distance from the LOWHC and from the Bishop's
Lodgings. During my daily work I spoke my words aloud,
and during my lonely nights in my walk-up, I listed my words
and made sentences with them, all against Canaan Johnson.
My wrath mounted and mounted and my rage grew like old
Moseses in Deuteronomy. But I waited and waited and kept
my distance, and my vocabulary fattened.

All while I was cleaning house, all while I was
vacuuming and a-polishing, I studied this situation and I was
delivering one long livid sermon to Canaan Johnson, no
doubt my masterpiece if it could have been heard. I would
not go near to the church except to clean it on Saturdays. I
owed this to the Lord and it was not for Savata and Canaan
Johnson; it was my tithe — and a way to hear things from
those around the LOWHC, my one thread of contact. I heard
that Savata had changed radically. She owned more and more
possessions. She preached in a streamlined dress of silk and
on it she wore a diamond star, I heard. It was her fairnesses
fault, I said. As we are the Black Jews, her difference became
her curse, where she could have made it her blessing. Look
how some other handicapped folks do — that Mordecai
Blake, he scuffles himself, sitting down, all over the sidewalks
of Great Neck in the name of the Church, and gets more
contributions than a man with legs awalking.

Time passed, with me housecleaning and tithing my
time to the LOWHC on Saturdays and hearing things and
studying what to do. I made several long distance calls to
Prince o'Light and he was my mainstay. He advised me to
bide out my time and not to slacken my faith. Once or twice

I so much wanted to see him, to talk to him, and even to
walk the avenue again with him like we did the night we
came so close together. Once I said, "I'm coming, Prince o'
Light, to walk and talk with thee as we did once"; but Prince
o' Light said, "do not come, Saint Sister Ruby Drew, we have
already walked that way together." Now what did he mean? I
thought. But then I seen that what he meant is that you can't
do it twice and get the same results; everything changes and is
never the same as 'twas; we do not step in the same river
twice, the water moves onc, etc. So I walked on alone, and
kept my feelings to myself, thank you Jesus. I bided my
time, stayed away by myself, so lonesome and aggrieved but
praying my way through. Every seldom I'd go over to the
Bishop's Lodgings and peer through the window at what was
happening. Always people ther, the Lodgings was alive with
activity. Canaan Johnson attracted into the Lodgings and
into the LOWHC a kind of intellectual element which,
conglomerated with the element which Savata attracted,
magic-hunters and show-hungry persons, made for a special
combination. Add to this the particular kind of woman that
hung around Canaan Johnson, glazing him like a chocolate
cake with their confections. The Light of the World
Quartette, four foolish females: two long-necked old maid
sisters that put on airs, a widow woman with horseteeth in
the widest mouth this side of Boca Chica, and a little flirt
thing that sung with a voice as small as a humming bird's and
in a register higher than that Lily Pons — the others all
drowned her out, I don't know why they kept her. Granted
they were very popular in the LOWHC, a hit from their first
appearance, and record crowd drawers. Still, their actions
around Canaan Johnson made you think they were his
harem. The Light of the World Quartette, *en masse*, was

perpetually in the Bishop's Lodgings; you couldn't peep in a window night or day and not see them there.

Then there was an old blind man full of self-pity that was always hanging around, for no good I assure you. He came for Canaan to teach him Hebrew and for Savata to read to him, so they all said. But he had big ears, filled like a cornucopia with gossip and illwinded news and it all just poured out of his mouth like a harvest of disaster and scandal. He explained that when the Lord takes away one organ he gives back another two-fold. He lived in his ears — though sometimes, I must say, in his fingers. His touch, as he felt out things around him, felt out where it didn't need to. He was a pincher, frankly. Now I don't mean to criticize human beings — and particularly God's own handicapped. But I do think this old codger exploited his blindness. I wouldn't get *near* him.

Add to this company two young brethren in the congregation, Jolly and Jamie — sound like twins but they wasn't — that Savata cottoned to. They begun to bring in more of the same, for Savata attracted them like a magnet. Jolly and Jamie and their friends were good souls, at bottom, and harmless as butterflies, goodness knows they meant no harm. But they brought into the LOWHC an element that lowered the church, I thought. I mean they made it kind of like a play party. They wore — I don't know, clothes like I never saw before, not even in Bloomingdales. All loud colours and tight. They laughed so much, and all alike. Oh they were sweet things, but not a serious bone in their bodies — not even a bone, seemed like. They took to Savata like a Queen, and then they adored Canaan Johnson and he liked them. Pretty soon they were having get-togethers at the Bishop's Lodgings and I noticed olives in the official ice-box which the

church bought with cold cash. Savata said they were show
people and as she had a past like their present, it was her
Bishop's duty to be of influence on them, to convert and save
them, even as she had been. She understood them. I couldn't
argue with this and I told myself, I am the mother of them
all, for I started the whole chain reaction of conversion from
shows and lewdities.

But was I the mother of what I saw one Saturday night
when after doing my cleaning at the LOWHC I dropped by
the Bishop's Lodgings unexpectedly? What I saw was nothing
fit for such a mother as I. The Boys, as they were called —
there was six of 'em now — Jolly and Jamie had brought in
four others — were cavorting outlandishly.

"They are showing us some of their numbers from their
act, Sister Ruby Drew," Savata purled out.

"Act?" I said.

In their show — the "Crystal Compote Revue" out in
the Bronx. The Boys were just all feathers and glitter with
such lashes on their eyes as would rival quills on a porcupine.

"You are sacred Black Jews by ancestry!" I lectured
out. "And you are corrupting up the heritage that your
forbears have handed down, black palm to black palm,
through the long ages, by your lewd activities!" I scourged
them.

"Oh rubbish!" grouched Canaan Johnson. "Why don't
you grow with the times, or put up a tent in the fields like
they did forty years ago, Ruby Drew."

"I believe in the Church Immutable!" I declared, using
back on Canaan a word I had armed myself with in my
vocabulary studying.

"The Church has always shown itself to be *mutable* to
the human condition," he cracked back. "That's its power."

Mutable was a word that threw me off the track of my sacred rage for a moment, because it brought before my eyes the face of a hateful girl whose name was Mutabel and I had no time to see *that* face of Mutabel's at such a moment. It was her iniquity interfering with my divine mission, like a ghost. She belonged to Satan, I knew for sure, now. Anyway, I spewed her face out of my eyes and looked upon The Boys again, and they were glittering and shuffling their feathers and making sounds with their mouth to mean their impatience, like pore old Mama used to do; and one that had a white feather in his hand kept fanning himself with it. All The Boys were in the skimpiest of costumes — sinful to see — I could not look upon them without being blinded by impiety.

Savata was backsliding, I could see that. Oh my God I cried out to myself, why must my life be one constant cauterizing out of wickedness, I'm so tarred. Soon as one is quelled, another one flares up — like a pack of mice in a big room. Give me some rest Oh Lord! I cried out to myself.

"Give me a Cream Soda, please," I asked Savata. "I am dry of mouth from God's toilsome work among backsliding mortals. And lend me Crosstown bus fare, your sister has not one red cent to her name."

I drank the soda that was like a cooling balm to my heated spirit — and fattening — and one of The Boys came feathering over to me and said, "Sister, we would all love to sing a sweet hymn with you when your throat is moistened by the Cream Soda. All of us boys do recognize that we are in need of spiritual cleansing once in a while, and we love to sing with you."

His esses literally pierced my eardrums they were so glassy. But he had a sweet face; really like a little innocent angel's, and right away I felt salvation of him and the others possible — for there is where we have to find the soul to be saved: in the sparkle and the featheriness of sin. I knew it once again. The other Boys come round me as I drunk my good Cream Soda and implored me, like innocent little children — so many feathers round me and brushing over me I felt like a big mother hen. I was inspired!

Oh that moment! Full of my Cream Soda, I leaned back and let out a cry on the first line of "He is My Blessed Love;" and oh I felt the love of God in my heart and his voice sang out through me and all The Boys sang out, and then Savata joined in — and Canaan Johnson watched and nodded, and I thought, "I was wrong, forgive me Saviour, I judged, I judged, there is good in everything."

And I was glad I come.

*from Ghost and Flesh*

# The White Rooster

HERE were two disturbances in Mrs. Marcy Samuels' life that were worrying her nearly insane. First, it was, and had been for two years now, Grandpa Samuels, who should have long ago been dead but kept wheeling around her house in his wheel chair, alive as ever. The first year he came to live with them it was plain that he was in good health and would probably live long. But during the middle of the second year he fell thin and coughing and after that there were some weeks when Mrs. Samuels and her husband, Watson, were sure on Monday that he would die and relieve them of him before Saturday. Yet he wheeled on and on, not ever dying at all.

The second thing that was about to drive Marcy Samuels crazy was a recent disturbance which grew and grew until it became a terror. It was a stray white rooster that crowed at her window all day long and, worst of all, in the early mornings. No one knew where he came from, but there he was, crowing to all the other roosters far and near—and they answering back in a whole choir or crowings. His shrieking was bad enough, but then he had to outrage her further by digging in her pansy bed. Since he first appeared to harass her, Mrs. Samuels had spend most of her day chasing him out of the flowers or throwing objects at him where he was, under her window, his neck stretched and strained in a perfectly blatant crow. After a week of this, she was almost frantic, as she told her many friends on the telephone or in town or from her back yard.

It seemed that Mrs. Samuels had been cursed with problems all her life and everyone said she had the unluckiest time of it. That a woman sociable and busy as Marcy Samuels should have her father-in-law, helpless in a wheel chair, in her house to keep and take care of was just a shame. And Watson, her husband, was no help at all, even though it was his very father who was so much trouble. He was a slow, patient little man, not easily ruffled. Marcy Samuels was certain that he was not aware that her life was so hard and full of trouble.

She could not stand at her stove, for instance, but what Grandpa Samuels was there, asking what was in the pot and smelling of it. She could not even have several of the women over without him riding in and out among them, weak as he was, as they chatted in confidence about this or that town happening, and making bright or ugly remarks about women and what they said, their own affairs. Marcy, as she often told Watson, simply could not stop Grandpa's mouth, could not stop his wheels, could not get him out of her way. And she was busy. If she was hurrying across a room to get some washing in the sink or to get the broom, Grandpa Samuels would make a surprise run out at her from the hall or some door and streak across in front of her, laughing fiendishly or shouting boo! and then she would leap as high as her bulbous ankles would lift her and scream, for she was a nervous woman and had so many things on her mind. Grandpa had a way of sneaking into things Marcy did, as a weevil slips into a bin of meal and bores around in it. He had a way of objecting to Marcy, which she sensed everywhere. He haunted her, pestered her. If she would be bending down to find a thing in her cupboard, she would suddenly sense some shadow over her and then it would be Grandpa Samuels, he would be there, touch her like a ghost in the ribs and frighten her so that she would bounce up and let out a scream. Then he would just sit and grin at her with an owlish face. All these things he did, added to the trouble it was for her to keep him, made Marcy Samuels sometimes want to kill Grandpa Samuels. He was everywhere upon her, like an evil spirit following her; and indeed there was a thing in him which scared her often, as if he was losing his mind or trying to kill her.

As for Grandpa, it was hard to tell whether he really had a wicked face or was deliberately trying to look mean, to keep Marcy troubled and to pay her back for the way she treated him. It may have been that his days were dull and he wanted something to happen, or that he remembered how he heard her fight with his son, her husband, at night in their room because Watson would not put him in a Home and get the house and Marcy free of him. "You work all day and you're not here with him like I am," she would whine. "And you're not man enough to put him where he belongs." He had been wicked in his day, as men are wicked, had drunk always and in all drinking places, had gambled and had got mixed up in some scrapes. But that was because he had been young and ready. He had never had a household, and the wife he finally got had long since faded away so that she might have been only a shadow from which this son, Watson, emerged, parentless. Then Grandpa had become an old wanderer, lo here lo there, until it all ended in this chair in which he was still a wanderer through the rooms of this house. He had a face which, although mischievous lines were scratched upon it and gave it a kind of devilish look, showed that somewhere there was abundant untouched kindness in him, a life which his life had never been able to use.

Marcy could not make her husband see that this house was cursed and tormented; and then to have a scarecrow rooster annoying her the length of the day and half the early morning was too much for Marcy Samuels. She had nuisances in her house and nuisances in her yard.

It was on a certain morning that Mrs. Samuels first looked out her kitchen window to see this gaunt rooster strutting white on the ground. It took her only a second to know that this was the rooster that crowed and scratched in her flowers and so the whole thing started. The first thing she did was to poke her blowsy head out her window and puff her lips into a ring and wheeze shooooooo! through it, fiercely. The white rooster simply did a pert leap, erected his flamboyantly combed head sharp into the air, chopped it about for a moment, and then started scratching vigorously in the lush bed of pansies, his comb slapping like a girl's pigtails.

Since her hands were wet in the morning sink full of dishes, Mrs. Samuels stopped to dry them imperfectly and then hurried out the back door, still drying her hands in her apron. Now she would get him, she would utterly destroy him if she could get her hands on him. She flounced out the door and down the steps and threw her great self wildly in the direction of the pansy bed, screaming shoo! shoo! go 'way! go 'way! and then cursed the rooster. Marcy Samuels must have been a terrible sight to any barnyard creature, her hair like a big bush and her terrible bosom heaving and falling, her hands thrashing the air. But the white rooster was not dismayed at all. Again he did a small quick hop, stuck his beak into the air, and stood firmly on his ground, his yellow

claw spread over the face of a purple pansy and holding it to
the ground imprisoned as a cat holds down a mouse. And
then a sound, a clear melodious measure, which Mrs. Samuels
thought was the most awful noice in the world, burst from
his straggly throat.

He was plainly a poorly rooster, thin as some sparrow,
his white feathers drooping and without lustre, his comb of
extravagant growth but pale and flaccid, hanging like a
wrinkled glove over his eye. It was clear that he had been run
from many a yard and that in fleeing he had torn his feathers
and so tired himself that whatever he found to eat in random
places was not enough to keep any flesh on his carcass. He
would not be a good eating chicken, Mrs. Samuels thought,
running at him, for he has no meat on him at all. Anyway, he
was not like a chicken but like some nightmare rooster from
Hades sent to trouble her. Yet he was most vividly alive in
some courageous way.

She threw a stone a him and at this he leaped and
screamed in fright and hurdled the shrubbery into a vacant
lot. Mrs. Samuels dashed to her violated pansy bed and began
throwing up loose dirt about the stems, making reparations.
This was no ordinary rooster in her mind. Since she had a
very good imagination and was, actually, a little afraid of
roosters anyway, the white rooster took on a shape of terror
in her mind. This was because he was so indestructible.
Something seemed to protect him. He seemed to dare her to
capture him, and if she threw a shoe out her window at him,
he was not challenged, but just let out another startling crow
at her. And in the early morning in a snug bed, such a
crowing is like the cry of fire! or an explosion in the brain.

It was around noon of that day that Mrs. Samuels, at
her clothesline, sighted Mrs. Doran across the hedge, at her

line, her long fingers fluttering over the clothespins like
butterflies trying to light there.

"That your rooster that's been in my pansy bed and
crows all the time, Mrs. Doran?"

"Marcy, it must be. You know we had two of them
intending to eat them for Christmas, but they both broke out
of the coop and went running away into the neighborhood.
My husband Carl just gave them up because he says he's not
going to be chasing any chickens like some farmer."

"Well then I tell you we can't have him here disturbing
us. If I catch him do you want him back?"

"Heavens no, honey. If you catch him, do what you
want to with him, we don't want him any more. Lord knows
where the other one is." And then she unfolded from her tub
a long limp outing gown and pinned it to the line by its
shoulders to let it hang down like an effigy of herself.

Mrs. Samuels noticed that Mrs. Doran was as casual
about the whole affair as she was the day she brought back
her water pitcher in several pieces, borrowed for a party and
broken by the cat. It made her even madder with the white
rooster. This simply means killing that white rooster, she told
herself as she went from her line. It means wringing his neck
until it is twisted clean from his breastbone—if we can catch
him; and I'll try—catch him and throw him in the chickenyard and hold him there until Watson comes home from
work and then Watson will do the wringing, not me. When
she came in the back door she was already preparing herself
in her mind for the killing of the white rooster, how she
would catch him and then wait for Waston to wring his
neck—if Watson actually could get up enough courage to do
anything at all for her.

In the afternoon around two, just as she was resting, she

heard a cawing and it was the rooster back again. Marcy bounded from her bed and raced to the window. "Now I will get him," she said severly.

She moved herself quietly to a bush and concealed herself behind it, her full-blown buttocks protruding like a monstrous flower in bud. Around the bush in a smiling innocent circle were the pansies, all purple and yellow faces, bright in the wind. When he comes scratching here, she told herself, and when he gets all interested in the dirt, I'll leap upon him and catch him sure.

Behind the bush she waited; her eyes watched the white rooster moving towards the pansy bed, pecking here and there in the grass at whatever was there and might be eaten. As she prepared herself to leap, Mrs. Samuels noticed the white hated face of Grandpa at the window. He had rolled his wheel chair there to watch the maneuvers in the yard. She knew at a glance that he was against her catching the white rooster. But because she hated him, she did not care what he thought. In fact she secretly suspected Grandpa and the rooster to be partners in a plot to worry her out of her mind, one in the house, the other in the yard, tantalizing her outside and inside; she wouldn't put it past them. And if she could destroy the rooster that was a terror in the yard she had a feeling that she would be in a way destroying a part of Grandpa that ws a trouble in her house. She wished she were hiding behind a bush to leap out upon *him* to wring *his* neck. He would not die, only wheel through her house day after day, asking for this and that, meddling in everything she did.

The rooster came to the pansy bed so serene, even in rags of feathers, like a beggar-saint, sure in his head of something, something unalterable, although food was unsure, even life. He came as if he knew suffering and terror, as if he

were alone in the world of fowls, far away from his flock,
alien and far away from any golden grain thrown by caring
hands, stealing a wretched worm or cricket from a foreign
yard. What made him so alive, what did he know? Perhaps as
he thrust the horned nails of his toes in the easy earth of the
flower bed he dreamed of the fields on a May morning, the
jeweled dew upon their grasses and the sun coming up like
the yolk of an egg swimming in an albuminous sky. And the
roseate freshness of his month when he was a tight-fleshed
slender-thighed cockerel, alert on his hill and the pristine
morning breaking all around him. To greet it with cascading
trills of crowings, tremulous in his throat, was to quiver his
thin red tongue in trebles. What a joy he felt to be of the
world of wordless creatures, where crowing or whirring of
wings or the brush of legs together said everything, said
praise, we live. To be of the grassy world where things blow
and bend and rustle; of the insect world so close to it that it
was known when the most insignificant mite would turn in
its minute course or an ant haul an imperceptible grain of
sand from its tiny cave.

And to wonder at the world and to be able to articulate
the fowl-wonder in the sweetest song. He knew time as the
seasons know it, being of time. He was tuned to the
mechanism of dusk and dawn, it may have been in his mind
as simple as the dropping of a curtain to close out the light or
the lifting of it to let light in upon a place. All he knew,
perhaps, was that there is a going round, and first light comes
ever so tinily and speck-like, as through the opening of a
stalk, when it is time. Yet the thing that is light breaking on
the world is morning breaking open, unfolding within him
and he feels it and it makes him chime, like a clock, at his
hour. And this is daybreak for him and he feels the daybreak

in his throat, and tells of it, rhapsodically, not knowing a single word to say.

And once he knew the delight of wearing red-blooded wattles hanging folded from his throat and a comb climbing up his forehead all in crimson horns to rise from him as a star, pointed. To be rooster was to have a beak hard and brittle as shell, formed just as he would have chosen a thing for fowls to pick grain or insect from their place. To be bird was to be of feathers and shuffle and preen them and to carry wings and arch and fold them, or float them on the wind, to be wafted, to be moved a space by them.

But Marcy Samuels was behind the bush, waiting, and while she waited her mind said over and over, "If he would die!" If he would die, by himself. How I could leap upon him, choke the life out of him. The rooster moved toward the pansies, tail feathers drooped and frayed. If he would die, she thought, clenching her fists. If I could leap upon him and twist his old wrinkled throat and keep out the breath.

At the window, Grandpa Samuels knew something terrible was about to happen. He watched silently. He saw the formidable figure of Mrs. Samuels crouching behind the bush, waiting to pounce upon the rooster.

In a great bounce-like movement, Mrs. Samuels suddenly fell upon the rooster, screaming, "If he would die!" And caught him. The rooster did not struggle, although he cawed out for a second and then meekly gave himself up to Mrs. Samuels. She ran with him to the chickenyard and stopped at the fence. But before throwing him over, she first tightened her strong hands around his neck and gritted her teeth, just to stop the breathing for a moment, to crush the crowing part of him, as if it were a little waxen whistle she could smash. Then she threw him over the fence. The white rooster lay over on his back, very tired and dazed, his yellow legs straight in the air, his claws clenched like fists and not moving, only trembling a little. The Samuels' own splendid golden cock approached the shape of feathers to see what this was, what had come over into his domain, and thought surely it was dead. He leaped upon the limp fuss of feathers and drove his fine spurs into the white rooster just to be sure he was dead. And all the fat pampered hens stood around gazing and casual in a kind of fowlish elegance, not really disturbed, only a bit curious, while the golden cock bristled his fine feathers and, feeling in himself what a thing of price and intrepidity he was, posed for a second like a statue imitating some splendid ancestor cock in his memory, to comment upon this intrusion and to show himself unquestionable master, his beady eyes all crimson as glass hat pins. It was apparent that his hens were proud of him and that in their eyes he had lost none of his prowess by not having himself captured the rooster, instead of Mrs. Samuels. And Marcy Samuels, so relieved, stood by the fence a minute showing something of the same thing in her that the hens showed, very viciously proud. Then she brushed her hands clean of the white rooster and marched victoriously to the house.

Grandpa Samuels was waiting for her at the door, a dare in his face, and said "Did you get him?"

"He's in the yard waiting until Watson comes home to kill him. I mashed the breath out of the scoundrel and he may be dead the way he's lying on his back in the chickenyard. No more crowing at my window, no more scratching in my pansy bed, I'll tell you. I've got one thing off my mind."

"Marcy," Grandpa said calmly and with power, "that

rooster's not dead that easily. Don't you know there's
something in a rooster that won't be downed? Don't you
know there's some creatures won't be dead easily?" And
wheeled into the living room.

But Mrs. Samuels yelled back from the kitchen,

"All you have to do is wring their necks."

All afternoon the big wire wheels of Grandpa Samuels'
chair whirled through room and room. Sometimes Mrs.
Samuels thought she would pull out her mass of wiry hair,
she got so nervous with the cracking of the floor under the
wheels. The wheels whirled around in her head just as the
crow of the rooster had burst in her brain all week. And then
Grandpa's coughing: he would, in a siege of cough, dig away
down in his throat for something troubling him there, and,
finally, seizing it as if the cough were a little hand reaching
for it, catch it and bring it up, the old man's phlegm, and spit
it quivering into a can which rode around with him on the
chair's footrest.

"This is as bad as the crowing of the white rooster,"
Mrs. Samuels said to herself as she tried to rest. "This is
driving me crazy" And just when she was dozing off, she
heard a horrid gurgling sound from the front bedroom where
Grandpa was. She ran there and found him blue in his face
and gasping.

"I'm choking to death with a cough, get me some water,
quick!" he murmured hoarsely. As she ran to the kitchen
faucet, Marcy had the picture of the white rooster in her
mind, lying breathless on his back in the chickenyard, his
thin yellow legs in the air and his claws closed and drooped
like a wilted flower. "If he would die," she thought. "If he
would strangle to death."

When she poured the water down his throat, Marcy

Samuels put her fat hand there and pressed it quite desperately as if the breath were a little bellows and she could perhaps stop it still just for a moment. Grandpa was unconscious and breathing laboriously. She heaved him out of his chair and to his bed, where he lay crumpled and exhausted. Then was when she went to the telephone and called Watson, her husband.

"Grandpa is very sick and unconscious and the stray rooster is caught and in the chickenyard to be killed by you," she told him. "Hurry home, for everything is just terrible."

When Marcy went back to Grandpa's room with her hopeful heart already giving him extreme unction, she had the shock of her life to find him not dying at all but sitting up in his bed with a face like a caught rabbit, pitiful yet daredevilish.

"I'm all right now, Marcy, you don't have to worry about *me*. You couldn't *kill* an old crippled man like me," he said firmly.

Marcy was absolutely spellbound and speechless, but when she looked out Grandpa's window to see the white rooster walking in the leaves, like a resurrection, she thought she would faint with astonishment. Everything was suddenly like a haunted house; there was death and then a bringing to life again all around her and she felt so superstitious that she couldn't trust anything or anybody. Just when she was sure she was going to lose her breath in a fainting spell, Watson arrived home. Marcy looked wild. Instead of asking about Grandpa, whether he was dead, he said, "There's no stray rooster in my chickenyard like you said, because I just looked." And when he looked to see Grandpa all right and perfectly conscious he was in a quandary and said they were playing a trick on a worried man.

"This place is haunted, I tell you," Marcy said, terrorized, "and you've got to do something for once in your life." She took him in the back room where she laid out the horror and the strangeness of the day before him. Watson, who was always calm and a little underspoken, said, "All right, pet, all right. There's only one thing to do. That's lay a trap. Then kill him. Leave it to me, and calm your nerves." And then he went to Grandpa's room and sat and talked to him to find out if he was all right.

For an hour, at dusk, Watson Samuels was scrambling in a lumber pile in the garage like a possum trying to dig out. Several times Mrs. Samuels inquired through the window by signs what he was about. She also warned him, by signs, of her fruit-jars stored on a shelf behind the lumber pile and to be careful. But at a certain time during the hour of building, as she was hectically frying supper, she heard a crash of glass and knew it was her Mason jars all over the ground, and cursed Watson.

When finally Mr. Samuels came in, with the air of having done something grand in the yard, they ate supper. There was the sense of having something special waiting afterwards, like a fancy dessert.

"I'll take you out in awhile and show you the good trap I built," Watson said. "That'll catch anything."

Grandpa, who had been silent and eating sadly as an old man eats (always as if remembering something heartbreaking), felt sure how glad they would be if they could catch *him* in the trap.

"Going to kill that white rooster, son?" he asked.

"It's the only thing to do to keep from making a crazy woman out of Marcy."

"Can't you put him in the yard with the rest of the

chickens when you catch him?" He asked this mercifully. "That white rooster won't hurt anybody."

"You've seen we can't keep him in there, Papa. Anyway, he's probably sick or got some disease."

"His legs are scaly. I saw that," Mrs. Samuels put in.

"And then he'd give it to my good chickens," said Mr. Samuels. "Only thing for an old tramp like that is to wring his neck and throw him away for something useless and troublesome."

When supper was eaten, Watson and Marcy Samuels hurried out to look at the trap. Grandpa rolled to the window and watched through the curtain. He watched how the trap lay in the moonlight, a small dark object like a box with one end open for something to run in, something seeking a thing needed, like food or a cup of gold beyond a rainbow, and hoping to find it here within this cornered space. "It's just a box with one side kicked out," he said to himself. "But it is a trap and built to snare and to hold." It looked lethal under the moon; it cast a shadow longer than itself and the open end was like a big mouth, open to swallow down. He saw his son and his son's wife—how they moved about the trap, his son making terrifying gestures to show how it would work, how the guillotine end would slide down fast when the cord was released from inside the house, and close in the white rooster, close him in and lock him there, to wait to have his neck wrung off. He was afraid, for Mrs. Samuels looked strong as a lion in the night, and how cunning his son seemed! He could not hear what they spoke, only see their gestures. But he heard when Mrs. Samuels pulled the string once, trying out the trap, and the top came sliding down with a swift clap when she let go. And then he knew how adroitly they could kill a thing and with what craftiness. He was sure he was no longer safe in this house, for after the rooster then certainly he would be trapped.

The next morning early the white rooster was there, crowing in a glittering scale. Grandpa heard Marcy screaming at him, threatening, throwing little objects through the window at him. His son Watson did not seem disturbed at all; always it was Marcy. But still the rooster crowed. Grandpa went cold and trembling in his bed. He had not slept.

It was a rainy day, ashen and cold. By eight o'clock it had settled down to a steady gray pour. Mrs. Samuels did not bother with the morning dishes. She told Grandpa to answer all phone calls and tell them she was out in town. She took her place at the window and held the cord in her hand.

Grandpa was so quiet. He rolled himself about ever so gently and tried not to cough, frozen in his throat with fear and a feeling of havoc. All through the house, in every room, there was darkness and doom, the air of horror, slaughter and utter finish. He was so full of terror he could not breathe, only gasp, and he sat leaden in his terror. He thought he heard footsteps creeping upon him to choke his life out, or a hand to release some cord that would close down a heavy door before him and lock him out of his life forever. But he would not keep his eyes off Marcy. He sat in the doorway, half obscured, and pecked at her, he watched her like a hawk.

Mrs. Samuels say by the window in a kind of ecstatic readiness. Everywhere in her was the urge to release the cord—even before the time to let it go, she was so passionately anxious. Sometimes she thought she could not trust her wrist, her fingers, they were so ready to let go, and then she changed the cord to the other hand. But her hands were so charged with their mission that they could have easily thrust a blade into a heart to kill it, or brought down mightily a hammer upon a head to shatter the skull in. Her hands had well and wantonly learned slaughter from her heart, had been thoroughly taught by it, as the heart whispers to its agents—hands, tongue, eyes—to do their action in their turn.

Once Grandpa saw her body start and tighten. She was poised like a huge cat, watching. He looked, mortified, through the window. It was a bird on the ground in the slate rain. Another time, because a dog ran across the yard, Mrs. Samuels jerked herself straight and thought, something comes, it is time.

And then it seemed there was a soft ringing in Grandpa's ears, almost like a delicate little jingle of bells or of thin glasses struck, and some secret thing told him in his heart that it was time. He saw Mrs. Samuels sure and powerful as a great beast, making certain, making ready without flinching. The white rooster was coming upon the grass.

He strode upon the watered grass all dripping with the rain, a tinkling sound all about him, the rain twinkling upon his feathers, forlorn and tortured. Yet even now there was a blaze of courage about him. He was meager and bedraggled. But he had a splendor in him. For now his glory came by being alone and lustreless in a beggar's world, and there is a time for every species to know lacklustre and loneliness where there was brightness and a flocking together, since there is a change in the way creatures must go to find their ultimate station, whether they fall old and lose blitheness, ragged and lose elegance, lonely and lose love; and since there is a shifting in the levels of understanding. But there is something in each level for all creatures, pain or wisdom or despair, and never nothing. The white rooster was coming upon the grass.

Grandpa wheeled so slowly and so smoothly towards Mrs. Samuels that she could not tell he was moving, that not one board cracked in the floor. And the white rooster moved toward the trap, closer and closer he moved. When he saw the open door leading to a dry place strewn with grain, he went straight for it, a haven suddenly thrown up before his eye, a warm dry place with grain. When he got to the threshold of the trap and lifted his yellow claw to make the final step, Grandpa Samuels was so close to Mrs. Samuels that he could hear her passionate breath drawn in a kind of lust-panting. And when her heart must have said, "Let go!" to her fingers, and they tightened spasmodically so that the veins stood turgid blue in her arm, Grandpa Samuels struck at the top of her spine where the head flares down into the neck and there is a little stalk of bone, with a hunting knife he had kept for many years. There was no sound, only the sudden sliding of the cord as it made a dip and hung loose in Marcy Samuels' limp hand. Then Grandpa heard the quick clap of the door hiting the wooden floor of the trap outside, and a faint crumpling sound as of a dress dropped to the floor when Mrs. Samuels' blowsy head fell limp on her breast. Through the window Grandpa Samuels saw the white rooster leap pertly back from the trap when the door came down, a little frightened. And then he let out a peal of crowings in the rain and went away.

Grandpa sat silent for a moment and then said to Mrs. Samuels, "You will never die any other way, Marcy Samuels, my son's wife, you are meant to be done away with like this. With a hunting knife."

And then he wheeled wildly away through the rooms of Marcy Samuels' house, feeling a madness all within him, being liberated, running free. He howled with laughter and rumbled like a runaway carriage through room and room, sometimes coughing in paroxysms. He rolled here and there in every room, destroying everything he could reach, he threw up pots and pans in the kitchen, was in the flour and sugar like a whirlwind, overturned chairs and ripped the upholstery in the living room until the stuffing flew in the air; and covered with straw and flour, white like a demented ghost, he flayed the bedroom wallpaper into hanging shreds; coughing and howling, he lashed and wrecked and razed until he thought he was bringing the very house down upon himself.

When Watson came home some minutes later to check on the success of his engine to trap the rooster and fully expecting to have to wring his neck, he saw at one look his house in such devastation that he thought a tornado had struck and demolished it inside, or that robbers had broken in. "Marcy! Marcy!" he called.

He found out why she did not call back when he discovered her by the window, cord in hand as though she had fallen asleep fishing.

"Papa! Papa!" he called.

But there was no calling back. In Grandpa's room Watson found the wheel chair with his father's wild dead body in it, his life stopped by some desperate struggle. There had obviously been a fierce spasm of coughing, for the big artery in his neck had burst and was still bubbling blood like a little red spring.

Then the neighbors all started coming in, having heard the uproar and gathered in the yard; and there was a dumbfoundedness in all their faces when they saw the ruins in Watson Samuels' house, and Watson Samuels standing there

in the ruins unable to say a word to any of them to explain
what had happened.

# Ghost And Flesh, Water And Dirt

**W**AS somebody here while ago acallin for you. . . .

*O don't say that, don't tell me who . . . was he fair and
had a wrinkle in his chin? I wonder was he the one . . .
describe me his look, whether the eyes were pale lightcolored
and swimmin and wild and shifty; did he bend a little at the
shoulders was his face agrievin what did he say where did he
go, whichaway, hush don't tell me; wish I could keep him
but I cain't, so go, go (but come back).*

Cause you know honey there's a time to go roun and
tell and there's a time to set still (and let a ghost grieve ya);
so listen to me while I tell, cause I'm in my time a tellin and
you better run fast if you don wanna hear what I tell, cause
I'm goin ta tell . . .

Dreamt last night again I saw pore Raymon Emmons, all
last night seen im plain as day. There uz tears in iz glassy eyes
and iz face uz all meltin away. O I was broken of my sleep
and of my night disturbed, for I dreamt of pore Raymon
Emmons live as ever.

He came on the sleepin porch where I was sleepin (and
he's there to stay) ridin a purple horse (like King was), and
then he got off and tied im to the bedstead and come and
stood over me and commenced iz talkin. All night long he uz
talkin and talkin, his speech (whatever he uz sayin) uz like

steam streamin outa the mouth of a kettle, streamin and
streamin and streamin. At first I said in my dream, 'Will you
do me the favor of tellin me just who in the world you can
be, will you please show the kindness to tell me who you can
be, breakin my sleep and disturbin my rest?" 'I'm Raymon
Emmons,' the steamin voice said, 'and I'm here to stay; putt
out my things that you've putt away, putt out my oatmeal
bowl and putt hot oatmeal in it, get out my rubberboots
when it rains, iron my clothes and fix my supper . . . I never
died and I'm here to stay.

*(Oh go way ole ghost of Raymon Emmons, whisperin in
my ear on the pilla at night; go way ole ghost and lemme be!.
Quit standin over me like that, all night standin there sayin
somethin to me . . . behave ghost of Raymon Emmons,
behave yoself and lemme be! Lemme get out and go roun,
lemme put on those big ole rubberboots and go clompin. . . .)*

Now you shoulda known that Raymon Emmons. *There*
was *somebody*, I'm tellin you. Oh he uz a bright thang, quick
'n fair, tall, about six feet, real lean and a devlish face full of
snappin eyes, he had eyes all over his face, didn't miss a
thang, that man, saw everthang; and a clean brow. He was a
rayroad man, worked for the Guff Coast Lines all iz life, our
house always smelt like a train.

When I first knew of him he was living at the
Boardinhouse acrost from the depot (oh that uz years and
years ago), and I uz in town and wearin my first pumps when
he stopped me on the corner and ast me to do him the favor
of tellin him the size a my foot. I was not afraid atall to look
at him and say the size a my foot uz my own affair and
would he show the kindness to not be so fresh. But when he
said I only want to know because there's somebody livin up
in New Waverley about your size and age and I want to send

a birthday present of some houseshoes to, I said that's different; and we went into Richardson's store, to the back where the shoes were, and tried on shoes till he found the kind and size to fit me and this person in New Waverley. I didn't tell im that the pumps I'uz wearin were Sistah's and not my size (when I got home and Mama said why'd it take you so long? I said it uz because I had to walk so slow in Sistah's pumps).

Next time I saw im in town (and I made it a point to look for im, was why I come to town), I went up to im and said do you want to measure my foot again Raymon Emmons, ha! And he said any day in the week I'd measure that pretty foot; and we went into Richardson's and he bought *me* a pair of white summer pumps with a pink tie (and I gave Sistah's pumps back to her). Mis Richardson said my lands Margy you buyin lotsa shoes lately, are you goin to take a trip (O I took a trip, and one I come back from, too).

We had other meetins and was plainly in love; and when we married, runnin off to Groveton to do it, everbody in town said things about the marriage because he uz thirty and I uz seventeen.

We moved to this house owned by the Picketts, with a good big clothesyard and a swing on the porch, and I made it real nice for me and Raymon Emmons, made curtains with fringe, putt jardinears on the front bannisters and painted the fern buckets. We furnished those unfurnished rooms with our brand new lives, and started goin along.

Between those years and this one I'm tellin about them in, there seems a space as wide and vacant and silent as the Neches River, with my life *then* standin on one bank and my life *now* standin on the other, lookin acrost at each other like two different people wonderin who the other can really be.

How did Raymon Emmons die? Walked right through a
winda and tore hisself all to smithereens. Walked right
through a second-story winda at the depot and fell broken on
the tracks—nothin much left a Raymon Emmons after he
walked through that winda—broken his crown, hon, broken
his crown. But he lingered for three days in Victry Hospital
and then passed, sayin just before he passed away, turning
towards me, 'I hope you're satisfied. . . .'

Why did he die? From grievin over his daughter and
mine, Chitta was her name, that fell off a horse they uz both
ridin on the Emmonses' farm. Horse's name was King and we
had im shot.

Buried im next to Chitta's grave with iz insurance, two
funerals in as many weeks, then set around blue in our house,
cryin all day and cryin half the night, sleep all broken and
disturbed of my rest, thinkin oh if he'd come knockin at that
door right now I'd let him in, oh I'd let Raymon Emmons in!
After he died, I set aroun sayin 'who's gonna meet all the
hours in a day with me, whatever is in each one—*all those
hours*—who's gonna be with me in the mornin, in the ashy
afternoons that we always have here, in the nights of lightnin
who's goan be lyin there, seen in the flashes and makin me
feel as safe as if he uz a lightnin rod (and honey he *wuz*);
who's gonna be like a light turned on in a dark room when I
go in, who's gonna be at the door when I open it, who's goin
to be there when I wake up or when I go to sleep, who's goin
to call my name? I cain't stand a life of just me and our
furniture in a room, who's gonna *be* with me?' Honey it's
true that you never miss water till the well runs dry, tiz truly
true.

Went to talk to the preacher, but he uz no earthly help,
regalin me with iz pretty talk, he's got a tongue that will trill
out a story pretty as a bird on a bobwire fence—but meanin
what?—sayin 'the wicked walk on every hand when the vilest
men are exalted'—and now what uz that mean?—; went to set
and talk with Fursta Evans in her Millinary Shop (who's had
her share of tumult in her sad life, but never shows it) but she
uz no good, sayin 'Girl pick up the pieces and go on . . . here
try on this real cute hat' (that woman had nothin but hats on
her mind—even though she taught me *my* life, grant cha
*that*—for brains she's got hats). Went to the graves on
Sundays carryin potplants and crying over the mounds, one
long wide one and one little un—how sad are the little graves
a childrun, children ought not to have to die it's not right to
bring death to childrun, they're just little toys grownups play
with or neglect (thas how some of em die, too, honey, but
won't say no more bout that); but all childrun go to Heaven
so guess it's best—the grasshoppers flying all roun me (they
say graveyard grasshoppers spit tobacco juice and if it gets in
your eye it'll putt your eye out) and an armadilla diggin in
the crepemyrtle bushes—sayin 'dirt lay light on Raymon
Emmons and iz child,' and thinkin 'all my life is dirt I've got
a famly of dirt.' And then I come back to set and scratch
around like an armadilla myself in these rooms, alone; but
honey that uz no good either.

And then one day, I guess it uz a year after my famly
died, there uz a knock on my door and it uz Fursta Evans
knockin when I opened it to see. And she said 'honey now
listen I've come to visit with you and to try to tell you
somethin: why are you so glued to Raymon Emmonses
memry when you never cared a hoot bout him while he was
on earth, you despised all the Emmonses, said they was just

trash, wouldn't go to the farm on Christmas or Thanksgivin, wouldn't set next to em in church, broke pore Raymon Emmons's heart because you'd never let Chitta stay with her grandparents and when you finely did the Lord punished you for bein so hateful by takin Chitta. Then you blamed it on Raymon Emmons, hounded im night and day, said he killed Chitta, drove im stark ravin mad. While Raymond Emmons was live you'd never even give him the time a day, wouldn't lift a hand for im, you never would cross the street for im, to you he uz just a dog in the yard, and you know it, and now that he's dead you grieve yo life away and suddenly fall in love with im.' Oh she tole me good and proper—said, 'you never loved im till you lost im, till it uz too late, said now set up and listen to me and get some brains in yo head, chile.' Said, 'cause listen honey, I've had four husbands in my time, two of em died and two of em quit me, but each one of em I thought was goin to be the *only* one, and I took each one for that, then let im go when he uz gone, kept goin roun, kept ready, we got to honey, left the gate wide open for anybody to come through, friend or stranger, ran with the hare and hunted with the hound, honey we got to *greet* life not grieve life,' is what she said.

'Well,' I said, 'I guess that's the way life is, you don't know what you have till you don't have it any longer, till you've lost it, till it's too late.'

'Anyway,' Fursta said, 'little cattle little care—you're beginning again now, fresh and empty handed, it's later and it's shorter, yo life, but go on from *here* not *there*,' she said. 'You've had one kind of a life, had a husband, putt im in iz grave (now leave im there!), had a child and putt her away, too; start over, hon the world don't know it, the world's fresh as ever—it's a new day, putt some powder on yo face and start goin roun. Get you a job, and try that; or take you a trip. . . .'

'But I got to stay in this house,' I said. 'Feel like I cain't budge. Raymon Emmons is here, live as ever, and I cain't get away from im. He keeps me fastened to this house.'

'Oh poot,' Fursta said, lightin a cigarette. 'Honey you're losing ya mine. Now listen here, put on those big ole rubberboots and go clompin, go steppin high and wide—cause listen here, if ya don't they'll have ya up in the Asylum at Rusk sure's as shootin, specially if you go on talkin about this ghost of Raymon Emmons the way you do.'

'But if I started goin roun, what would people say?'

'You can tell em its none of their beeswax. Cause listen honey, the years uv passed and are passing and you in ever one of em, passin too, and not gettin any younger—yo hair's gettin bunchy and the lines clawed roun yo mouth and eyes by the glassy claws of crying sharp tears. We got to paint ourselves up and go on, young *outside*, anyway—cause listen honey the sun comes up and the sun crosses over and *goes down*—and while the sun's up we got to get on that fence and crow. Cause night muss fall—and then thas all. Come on, les go roun; have us a Sataday night weddin ever Sataday night; forget this old patched-faced ghost I hear you talkin about. . . .'

'In this town?' I said. 'I hate this ole town, always rain fallin—'cept this ain't rain it's rainin, Fursta, it's rainin mildew. . . .'

'O deliver me!' Fursta shouted out, and putt out her cigarette, 'you don't do. Are you afraid you'll *melt*?'

'I wish I'd melt—and run down the drains. Wish I uz rain, fallin on the dirt of certain graves I know and seepin down into the dirt, could lie in the dirt with Raymon Emmons on one side and Chitta on the other. Wish I uz dirt. . . .'

'I wish you are just crazy,' Fursta said. 'Come on, you're gonna take a trip. You're gonna get on a train and take a nonstop trip and get off at the end a the line and start all over again new as a New Year's Baby, baby. I'm gonna see to that.'

'Not on no train, all the king's men couldn't get me to ride a train again, no siree. . . .'

'Oh no train my foot,' said Fursta.

'But what'll I use for money please tell me,' I said.

'With Raymon Emmons's insurance of course—it didn't take all of it to bury im, I know. Put some acreage tween you and yo past life, and maybe some new friends and scenery too, and pull down the shade on all the water that's gone under the bridge; and come back here a new woman. Then if ya want tew you can come into my millinary shop with me.'

'Oh,' I said, 'is the world still there? Since Raymon Emmons walked through that winda seems the whole world's gone, the whole world went out through that winda when he walked through it.'

Closed the house, sayin 'goodbye ghost of Raymon Emmons,' bought my ticket at the depot, deafenin my ears to the sound of the tickin telegraph machine, got on a train and headed west to California. Day and night the trainwheels on the traintracks said *Raymon Emmons Raymon Emmons Raymon Emmons*, and I looked through the winda at dirt and desert, miles and miles of dirt, thinking I wish I uz dirt I wish I uz dirt. O I uz vile with grief.

In California the sun was out, wide, and everybody and everthing lighted up; and oh honey the world *was* still there. I decided to stay awhile. I started my new life with Raymon Emmons's insurance money. It uz in San Diego, by the ocean and with mountains of dirt standin gold in the blue waters. A war had come. I was alone for awhile, but not for long. Got me a job in an airplane factory, met a lotta girls, met a lotta men. I worked in fusilodges.

There uz this Nick Natowski, a brown clean Pollock from Chicargo, real wile, real Satanish. What kind of a life did he start me into? I don't know how it started, but it did, and in a flash we uz everwhere together, dancin and swimmin and *everything*. He uz in the war and in the U.S. Navy, but we didn't think of the war or of water. I just liked him tight as a glove in iz uniform, I just liked him laughin, honey, I just liked him *ever* way he was, and that uz all I knew. And then one night he said, 'Margy I'm goin to tell you somethin, goin on a boat, be gone a long long time, goin in a week.' Oh I cried and had a nervous fit and said, 'Why do you have to go when there's these thousands of others all aroun San Diego that could go?' and he said, 'We're goin away to Coronada for that week, you and me, and what happens there will be enough to keep and save for the whole time we're apart.' We went, honey, Nick and me, to Coronada, I mean we really *went*. Lived like a king and queen—where uz my life behind me that I thought of onct and a while like a story somebody was whisperin to me?—laughed and loved and I cried; and after that week at Coronada, Nick left for sea on his boat, to the war, sayin I want you to know baby I'm leavin you my allotment.

I was blue, so blue, all over again, but this time it uz diffrent someway, guess cause I uz blue for somethin live this time and not dead under dirt, I don't know; anyway I kept goin roun, kept my job in fusilodges and kept goin roun. There was this friend of Nick Natowski's called George, and we went together some. 'But why doesn't Nick Natowski write me, George?' I said. 'Because he cain't yet,' George said, 'but just wait and he'll write.' I kept waitin but no letter ever came, and the reason he didn't write when he could of, finely, was because his boat was sunk and Nick Natowski in it.

Oh what have I ever done in this world, I said, to send my soul to torment? Lost one to dirt and one to water, makes my life a life of mud, why was I ever put to such a test as this O Lord, I said. I'm goin back home to where I started, gonna get on that train and backtrack to where I started from, want to look at dirt awhile, can't stand to look at water. I rode the train back. Somethin drew me back like I'd been pastured on a rope in California.

Come back to this house, opened it up and aired it all out, and when I got back you know who was there in that house? That ole faithful ghost of Raymon Emmons. He'd been there, waitin, while I went aroun, in my goin roun time, and was there to have me back. While I uz gone he'd covered everthing in our house with the breath a ghosts, fine ghost dust over the tables and chairs and a spread of ghost lace over my bed on the sleepinporch.

Took me this job in Richardson's Shoe Shop (this town's big now and got money in it, the war 'n oil made it rich, ud never know it as the same if you hadn't known it before; and Fursta Evans married to a rich widower), set there fittin shoes on measured feet all day—it started in a shoestore measurin feet and it ended that way—can you feature that? Went home at night to my you-know-what.

Comes ridin onto the sleepinporch ever night regular as clockwork, ties iz horse to the bedstead and I say hello Raymon Emmons and we start our conversation. Don't ask me what he says or what I say, but ever night is a night full of talkin, and it lasts the whole night through. Oh onct in a while I get real blue and want to hide away and just set with Raymon Emmons in my house, cain't budge, don't see daylight nor dark, putt away my wearin clothes, couldn't walk outa that door if my life depended on it. But I set real still and let it all be, claimed by that ghost until he unclaims me—and then I get up and go roun, free, and that's why I'm here, settin with you here in the Pass Time Club, drinkin this beer and tellin you all I've told.

Honey, why am I tellin all this? Oh all our lives! So many things to tell. And I keep em to myself a long long time, tight as a drum, won't open my mouth, just set in my blue house with that ole ghost agrievin me, until there comes a time of tellin, a time to tell, a time to putt on those big ole rubberboots.

Now I believe in *tellin*, while we're live and goin roun; when the tellin time comes I say spew it out, we just got to tell things, things in our lives, things that've happened, things we've fancied and things we dream about or are haunted by. Cause you know honey the time to shut yo mouth and set moultin and mildewed in yo room, grieved by a ghost and fastened to a chair, comes back roun again, don't worry honey, it comes roun again. There's a time ta tell and a time ta set still ta let a thost grieve ya. So listen to me while I tell, cause I'm in my time a tellin, and you better run fast if you don wanna hear what I tell, cause I'm goin ta tell. . . .

The world is changed, let's drink ower beer and have us a time, tell and tell and tell, let's get that hot bird in a cole bottle tonight. Cause next time you think you'll see me and hear me tell, you won't: I'll be flat where I cain't budge again, like I wuz all that year, settin and hidin way . . . until

the time comes roun again when I can say oh go way ole
ghost of Raymon Emmons, go way ole ghost and lemme be!

Cause I've learned this and I'm gonna tell ya: there's a
time for live things and a time for dead, for ghosts and for
flesh 'n bones: all life is just a sharin of ghosts and flesh. Us
humans are part ghost and part flesh—part fire and part
ash—but I think maybe the ghost part is the longest lastin,
the fire blazes but the ashes last forever. I had fire in
California (and water putt it out) and ash in Texis (and it
went to dirt); but I say now, while I'm tellin you, there's a
world both places, a world where there's ghosts and a world
where there's flesh, and I believe the real right way is to take
our worlds, of ghosts or of flesh, take each one as they come
and take what comes in em: take a ghost and grieve with im,
settin still; and take the flesh 'n bones and go roun; and even
run out to meet what worlds come in to our lives, strangers
(like you), and ghosts (like Raymon Emmons) and lovers
(like Nick Natowski) . . . and be what each world wants us to
be.

And I think that ghosts, if you set still with em long
enough, can give you over to flesh 'n bones; and that flesh 'n
bones, if you go roun when it's time, can send you back to a
faithful ghost. One provides the other.

Saw pore Raymon Emmons all last night, all last night
seen im plain as day.

*from The Faces of Blood Kindred*

# Old Wildwood

ON a soft morning in May, at the American Express in Rome, the grandson was handed a letter; and high up on the Spanish Steps he sat alone and opened the letter and read its news. It was in his mother's hand:

"Well, your grandaddy died two days ago and we had his funeral in the house in Charity. There were so many flowers, roses and gladiolas and every other kind, that the front porch was filled with them, twas a sight to see. Then we took him to the graveyard where all the rest are buried and added his grave, one more, to the rest.

"At the graveyard your father suddenly walked out and stood and said the Lord's Prayer over his daddy's grave, as none of the Methodists in the family would hear a Catholic priest say a Catholic prayer, nor the Catholics in the family allow a Methodist one; and your grandaddy was going to be left in his grave without one holy word of any kind. But both were there, priest and preacher, and I said what a shame that your poor old daddy has to go to earth without even 'Abide with Me' sung by a soloist. His own begotten children marrying without conscience into this church and that, confounding their children as to the nature of God, caused it all, and there it was to see, clear and shameful, at the graveyard. Then all of a sudden your two great aunts, my mother's and your grandmother's sweet old sisters, Ruby and

Saxon Thompson, one blind and the other of such strutted ankles from Bright's Disease as could barely toddle, started singing 'Just As I Am Without One Plea,' and many joined in, it was so sweet and so sad and so peaceful to hear. Then we all walked away and left your grandaddy in his grave."

The grandson lifted his eyes from the letter and they saw an ancient foreign city of stone. So an old lost grandfather, an old man of timber, had left the world. He folded the letter and put it in his pocket. Then he leaned back and settled upon the pocked stone of the worn steps, supporting himself upon the opened palm of his hand. He rested a little, holding the letter, thinking how clear pictures of what had troubled his mind always came to him in some sudden, quiet ease of resting. He considered, as a man resting on stone, his grandfather.

Yes, he thought, the little old grandfather had the animal grace and solitary air of an old mariner about him, though he was a lumberman and purely of earth. His left leg was shorter than his right, and the left foot had some flaw in it that caused the shoe on it to curl upwards. The last time the grandson had seen his grandfather was the summer day when, home on leave from the Navy, and twenty-one, he had come out into the back yard in his shining officer's uniform to find his grandfather sitting there snowy-headed and holding his cap in his hand. Grandfather and grandson had embraced and the grandfather had wept. How so few years had changed him, the grandson had thought that afternoon: so little time had whitened his head and brought him to quick tears: and the grandson heard in his head the words of a long time back, spoken to him by his grandfather that night in Galveston, "Go over into Missi'ppi one day and see can you find your kinfolks . . ."

Where had the grandfather come from, that summer afternoon? Where had he been all these years? The grandson had scarcely thought of him. And now, suddenly, on that summer day of leave, he had heard his mother call to his father, "Your *daddy's* here," with an intonation of shame; and then his mother had come into his room and said, "Son, your grandaddy's here. Go out in the back yard and see your grandaddy."

When he had put on his uniform and stepped into the yard, there he saw the white-headed little man sitting on the bench. And there, resting on the grass and lying a little on its side as though it were a separate being, curled and dwarfed, was his grandfather's crooked foot, old disastrous companion.

The grandfather was an idler and had been run away from home, it was said, by his wife and children time and time again, and the last time for good; and where did he live and what did he do? Later, on the day of his visit and after he had gone away, the grandson's mother had confessed that she knew her husband went secretly to see his father somewhere in the city and to give him money the family had to do without. It was in a shabby little hotel on a street of houses of women and saloons that his father and his grandfather met and talked, father and son.

As he sat with his grandfather in the yard on the white bench under the camphor tree that summer, and now on this alien stone, the grandson remembered that the first time he had known his grandfather was on the trip to Galveston where they went to fish—the grandson was fourteen—and how lonesome he was there with this little old graying limping stranger who was his grandfather and who was wild somewhere that the grandson could not surmise, only fear.

Who was this man tied to him by blood through his father and who, though he strongly resembled his father, seemed an alien, not even a friend. The grandfather had sat on the rocks and drunk whiskey while the grandson fished; and though he did not talk much, the grandson felt that there was a constant toil of figuring going on in the old man as he looked out over the brown Gulf water, his feet bare and his shoes on the rock, one crooked one by one good one. On the rock the boy gazed at the bad foot for a long, long time, more often than he watched the fishing line, as though the foot on the rock might be some odd creature he had brought up from the water and left on the rock to perish in the sun. At night he watched it too, curled on the cot in the moonlight as his grandfather slept, so that he came to know it well on both rock and cot and to think of it as a special kind of being in itself. There on the rock, as on the cot, the bad foot was the very naked shape of the shoe that concealed it. It seemed lifeless there on the rock, it was turned inwards toward the good foot as though to ask for pity from it or to caricature it. The good foot seemed proud and aloof and disdainful, virile and perfectly shaped.

On the rock, the grandfather was like a man of the sea, the grandson thought, like a fisherman or a boat captain. His large Roman head with its bulging forehead characteristic of his children shone in the sun; and his wide face was too large for his small and rather delicate body, lending him a strangely noble bearing, classic and Bacchian. There was something deeply kind and tender in this old gentleman grandfather barefooted on the rock, drinking whiskey from the bottle. The grandson felt the man was often at the point of speaking to him of some serious thing but drank it all away again out of timidity or respect.

Each night they straggled back to their room in a cheap Gulf-front cabin full of flies and sand, and the grandson would help his grandfather into his cot where he would immediately fall to sleep. Then the grandson would lie for a long time watching his grandfather breathe, his graying curly hair tousled over his strutted forehead, and watching the sad foot that sometimes flinched on the sheet with fatigue, for it was a weak foot, he thought. Considering this man before him, the grandson thought how he might be a man of wood, grown in a wilderness of trees, as rude and native and unblazed as a wildwood tree. He held some wilderness in him, the very sap and seed of it. Then, half fearing the man, the grandson would fall asleep, with the thought and the image of the blighted foot worrying him. He was always afraid of his grandfather, no doubt because of the whiskey, but certainly for deeper, more mysterious reasons which he could not find out in this man who was yet so respectful to him.

One night after the grandfather had been drinking on the rock all day, he had drunk some more in the cabin and finally, sitting on the side of his cot, he had found the words he had to say to the grandson. He had spoken to him clearly and quietly and in such a kind of flowing song that the words might have been given him by another voice whispering him what to say.

"We all lived in Missi'ppi," was the way he began, quietly, to speak. "And in those days wasn't much there, only sawmills and wildwoods of good rich timber, uncut and unmarked, and lots of good Nigras to help with everything, wide airy houses and broad fields. It all seems now such a good day and time, though we didn't count it for much then. Your granny and I moved over out of Missi'ppi and into Texas, from one little mill town to another, me blazing timber and then cutting it, counting it in the railroad cars, your granny taking a new baby each time, seems like, but the same baby buggy for each—if we'd have named our children after the counties they were borned in, all twelve of them, counting the one that died in Conroe, you'd have a muster roll of half the counties of Texas—all borned in Texas; but not a one ever went back to Missi'ppi, nor cared. Twas all wildwood then, son, but so soon gone.

"I had such man's strength then, the kind that first my grandfather broke wilderness with into trail and clearing, hewed houses and towns out of timber with, the kind his grandsons used to break the rest. Why I fathered twelve children in the state of Texas and fed them on sweet milk and kidney beans and light bread and working twelve hours a day—mill and railroad—working Nigras and working myself and raising a family of barefooted towheads chasing the chickens and climbing the trees and carrying water, playing tree tag in the dirt yard stained with mulberries. Your granny wasn't deaf then, had better hearing than most, could hear the boll weevils in the cotton, could listen that well. We all slept all over the house, beds never made, always a baby squalling in the kitchen while your granny cooked, or eating dirt where it sat in the shade as your granny did the washing in the washpot on the fire with Nigras helping and singing, or riding the hip of one of the big girls or boys . . . my children grew up on each other's hips and you could never tell it now the way they live and treat each other.

"I didn't have any schooling, but my grandfather was a schoolteacher and broke clearing and built a log schoolhouse and taught in it—it still stands, I hear tell, in Tupolo—and lived to start a university in Stockton, Missi'ppi; was a Peabody and the Peabodys still live all over Missi'ppi, go in there and

you'll find Peabodys all over Missi'ppi. You know there's a
big bridge of steel over the Missi'ppi River at Meridian; that's
a Peabody, kin to me and kin to you. Another one, John
Bell, built a highway clean to the Louisiana line and starting
at Jackson; that's some of your kinfolks, old John Bell, such
a fine singing man, a good voice and pure black-headed
Irishman with his temper in his eyes. Called him Cousin Jack,
he was adopted, and just here in Galveston, to tell you the
truth, I've been wondering again who from; I've wondered
often about John Bell all these year, studied him time and
again. When I came he was already in our family, running
with the other children in the yard, seems like, when I first
saw him, and we all called him Cousin Jack, and all of my
family, brother and sister and even my own children, John
Bell was the best friend ever in this world to me. Aw, John
Bell's been heavy on my mind—John Bell! He was one to go
to. Cousin Jack was not ascared of anything, brave everywhere he went and not ascared of hard work, spit on his
hands and went right in. Went to work at fourteen and
helped the family. Was a jolly man and full of some of the
devil, too, and we raised a ruckus on Saturday nights when
we was young men together, we'd dance till midnight, court
the girls on the way home and come on home ourselves
singing and in great spirits. John Bell! Fishing and singing on
the river with a pint of bourbon in our hip pocket and a
breath of it on the bait for good luck. But something always
a little sad about John Bell, have never known what it could
be. Maybe it was his being adopted. He knew that; they told
him. But it was more than that. Then he married Nellie
Clayton, your Granny's niece, and I have never seen him
again. He built a highway clean through the state of Missi'ppi
and I always knew he would amount to something. Died in

1921, and now his children are all up and grown in Missi'ppi. They are some of the ones to look for. Find the Bells.

"Time came when all the tree country of East Texas was cut, seemed like no timber left, and new ways and new mills. I brought all my family to Houston, to work for the Southern Pacific. Some was married and even had babies of their own, but we stayed together, the whole kit and kaboodle of us, all around your granny. In the city of Houston we found one big old house and all lived in it. Then the family began to sunder apart, seemed like, with some going away to marry and then coming home again bringing husband or wife. I stayed away from home as much as I could, to have some peace from all the clamoring among my children. I never understood my children, son, could never make them out, my own children; children coming in and going out, half their children living there with this new husband and that, and the old husbands coming back to make a fuss, and one, Grace's, just staying on there, moved in and wouldn't ever leave, is still there to this day; and children from all husbands and wives playing all together in that house, with your granny deaf as a doornail and calling out to the children to mind, and wanting care, but would never leave and never will, she'll die in that house with all of them around her, abusing her, too, neither child nor grandchild minding her. I just left, son, and went to live in a boarding house. I'd go home on Sundays and on Easters and on Christmas, but not to stay. There's a time when a person can't help anything any more, anything. Still, they would come to me, one or another of my sons and daughters, but not to see how I was or to bring me anything, twas to borrow money from me. They never knew that I had lost my job with the S.P. because I drank a little whiskey.

"And I never went to any church, son, but I'm fifty years of age and I believe in the living God and practice the Golden Rule and I hope the Lord'll save me from my sins. But I never had anybody to go to, for help or comfort, and I want you to know your father didn't either, never had anybody to go to. But I want you to know you do, and I will tell you who and where so you will always know. I don't want you ever to know what it is not to have anybody to go to.

"So when you get to be a young man I hope you'll go over into Missi'ppi and see can you find your blood kinfolks. Tell them your grandaddy sent you there. Haven't been over there myself for thirty years, kept meaning to but just never did. Now I guess I never will. But you go, and when you go, tell them you are a Peabody's grandson. They're all there, all over there, all over Missi'ppi; look for the Peabodys and for the Claytons and look for the Bells . . ."

After the grandfather had finished his story, he sat still on his cot, looking down as if he might be regarding his bare crooked foot. The grandson did not speak or ask a question but he lay quietly thinking about it all, how melancholy and grand the history of relations was. Then, in a while, he heard his grandfather get up softly, put on his crooked shoe and the good one, and go out, thinking he was asleep. He has gone to find him John Bell, the grandson thought. The creaking of his bad shoe and the rhythm of his limp seemed to the grandson to repeat his grandfather's words: Peabodys and the Claytons and the Bells.

The grandson did not sleep while his grandfather was gone. He was afraid, for the tides of the Gulf were swelling against the sea wall below the cabin; yet he thought how he no longer feared his grandfather, for now that he had spoken to him so quietly and with such love he felt he was something of his own. He loved his grandfather. Yet now that he had been brought to love what he had feared, he was cruelly left alone in the whole world with this love, it seemed, and was that the way love worked?—with the unknown waters swelling and falling close to the bed where he lay with the loving story haunting him? There was so much more to it all, to the life of men and women, than he had known before he came to Galveston just to fish with his grandfather, so much in just a man barefooted on a rock and drinking whiskey in the sun, silent and dangerous and kin to him. And then the man had spoken and made a bond between them and brought a kind of nobility of forest, something like a shelter of grandness of trees over it all. The tree country! The grandson belonged to an old, illustrious bunch of people of timber with names he could now name, all a busy, honorable and worthy company of wilderness breakers and forest blazers, bridge builders and road makers, and teachers, Claytons and Peabodys and Bells, and the grandfather belonged to them, too, and it was he who had brought all the others home to him, his grandson. Yet the grandfather seemed an orphan. And now for the first time, the grandson felt the deep, free sadness of orphanage; and he knew he was orphaned, too. That was the cruel gift of his grandfather, he thought. The crooked foot! John Bell!

In this loneliness he knew, at some border where land turned into endless water, he felt himself to be the only one alive in this moment—where were all the rest?—in a land called Mississippi, called Texas, where? He was alone to do what he could do with it all and oh what to do would be some daring thing, told or performed on some shore where two ancient elements met, land and water, and touched each other and caused some violence of kinship between two orphans, and with heartbreak in it. What to do would have the quiet, promising dangerousness of his grandfather on the rock in it, it would have the grave and epic tone of his grandfather's ultimate telling on the side of the cot under one light globe in a mist of shoreflies in a sandy transient roof of revelation while the tide washed at the very feet of teller and listener. And what to do would have the feeling of myth and mystery that he felt as he had listened, as though when he listened he were a rock and the story he heard was water swelling and washing over generations and falling again, like the waters over the rock when the tide came in.

Suddenly he heard footsteps, and when the door opened quietly he saw his grandfather and a woman behind him. They came in the room and the woman whispered, "You didn't tell me that a kid was here."

"He's asleep, John Bell," the grandfather whispered.

Something began between the two, between the grandfather and the woman, and the grandson feigned sleep. But he watched through the lashes of his half-closed eyes as through an ambush of grass the odd grace of his grandfather struggling with the woman with whom he seemed to be swimming through water, and he heard his grandfather's low growl like a fierce dog on the cot, and he saw his grandfather's devil's foot treading and gently kicking, bare in the air, so close to him that he could have reached out to touch it. And then he knew that the foot had a very special beauty and grace of moment, a lovely secret performance hidden in it that had seemed a shame on his person and a flaw upon the rock. It had something, even, of a bird's movements in it. It was the crooked foot that was the source and the meaning of the strange and lovely and somehow delicate disaster on the bed; and it was that shape and movement that the grandson took for his own to remember.

John Bell!

The two people drank out of a bottle without saying a word, but they were celebrating something they had come through, as if they had succeeded in swimming, with each other's help, a laborious dangerous distance; and then they rose to leave the room together. But at the door, the grandfather called softly as he lifted the bottle once more to his mouth, "For John Bell . . . ," and the name rang deeply over the dark room like the tone of a bell upon the sea.

When they were gone, the grandson rose and looked out the window and saw the water with a horned moon over it and smelled the limey odors of shrimp, saw the delicate swaying starry lights of fishing boats; and there in the clear light of the moon he saw the rock he and his grandfather fished on. The tide was climbing over it and slipping back off it as if to cover it with a sighing embrace, like a body, as if to pull the rock, for a swelling moment, to its soft and caressing bosom of water; and there was a secret bathing of tenderness over the very world like a dark rock washed over with moonlit sea water and whiskey and tenderness and the mysteriousness of a grandfather, of an old story, an old ancestor of whom the grandson was afraid again. Now the grandfather seemed to the grandson to have been some old sea being risen out of the waters to sit on a rock and to tell a tale in a stranger's room, and disappear. Would he ever come again to fish on the rock in the Gulf and to snore on the cot in the cabin? But as he looked at the world of rock and tide and moon, in the grandson's head the words of a pioneer sounded, quiet and plaintive and urgent: Go over into Missi'ppi when you get to be a young man and see can you

find your kinfolks, son. Look for the Claytons and look for
the Peabodys and look for the Bells, all in there, all over
Missi'ppi . . . And the bell-rung deepness of a name called
sounded in the dark room.

*John Bell!*

There in the room, even then, alone and with the wild
lovely world he knew, tidewater and moonlight tenderly
tormenting the rock outside, and inside the astonishing
delicate performance tormenting the room, and the shape of
the foot on both room and rock, the grandson thought how
he would do, in his time, some work to bring about through
an enduring rock-silence a secret performance with something, some rock-force, some tide-force, some lovely, hearty,
fine wildwood wildwater thing always living in him through
his ancestry and now brought to sense in him, that old gamy
wilderness bequeathed him; how shaggy-headed, crooked-
footed perfection would be what he would work for, some
marvelous, reckless and imperfect loveliness, proclaiming
about the ways of men in the world and all that befell them,
all that glorified, all that damned them, clearing and covering
over and clearing again, on and on and on.

He went back to his cot and lay upon his young back.
Not to go to sleep! but to stay awake with it all, whatever,
whatever it was, keeping the wilderness awake in this and
many more rooms, breathing seawind and pinesap. Because—
now he felt sure— the thing to do about it all and with it all
would be in some performance of the senses after long silence
and waiting—of the hair that would grow upon his chest like
grass and of the nipples of his breast, of the wildwood in his
seed and the sappy sweat of the crease of his loins, of the
saltwater of his tears, the spit of his palms, the blistering of
the blazer's axehandle, all mortal stuff. To keep wilderness

awake and wild and never sleeping, in many rooms in many places was his plan in Galveston, and the torment that lay ahead for him would come, and it would hold him wakeful through nights of bitter desire for more than he could ever name, but for some gentle, lovely and disastrous heartbreak of men and women in this world. And in that room that held the history of his grandfather, the little poem of his forebears and the gesture of the now beautiful swimming and soaring crooked foot, he knew for himself that there would be, or he would make them, secret rooms in his life holding, like a gymnasium, the odors of mortal exertion, of desperate tournament, a violent contest, a hardy, laborious chopping, manual and physical and involving the strength in his blistering hands and the muscles of his heaving back, all the blazer's work, the pioneer's blazing hand! Or places upon rocks of silence where an enigma lay in the sun, dry and orphaned and moribund until some blessed tide eventually rose and caressed it and took it to its breast as if to whisper, "Belong to me before I slide away," and what was silent and half-dead roused and showed its secret  performance: that seemed to be the while history of everything, the secret, possible performance in everything that was sliding, sliding away.

Finally, his breast aching and its secret that lived there unperformed, but with the trembling of some enormous coming thrill, the distant disclosure of some vision, even, of some glimmering company of humanity of his yearning with whom to perform some daring, lovely, heartbroken and disastrous history; and with terror of listener and sadness of teller, the grandson fell alone to sleep and never heard his grandfather come back to his cot, that night in Galveston.

Now they had buried the grandfather. Bury the good man of wilderness, he thought; bury in Texas dirt the crooked foot that never walked again on the ground of Missi'ppi where mine has never been set. And find him John Bell in the next world.

His hand upon which he had rested was aching and he relieved it of his weight and sat upon the solid slab of ancient Travertine stone. There, engraved in the palm of the hand he had leaned on, was the very mark and grain of the stone, as though his hand were stone. He would not have a hand of stone! He would carry a hand that could labor wood and build a house, trouble dirt and lay a highway, and blaze a trail through leaf and bramble; and a hand that could rot like wood and fall into dust.

And then the grandson thought how all the style and works of stone had so deeply troubled him in this ancient city, and how he had not clearly know until now that he loved wood best and belonged by his very secret woodsman's nature to old wildwood.

# A People Of Grass

HE maundered about the city of Rome all day, misplaced. It was May, cold and dark and rainy, a bad spring, a cursed spring. Blossoms were late, crimped by cold and the pale touch of cold sun. He had left a cold room on whose worn floor of ancient tiles were sensual figures of faded crimson grapes and purple pears that stung bare feet with chill, and where a wan fire in a smoky fireplace did not warm naked flesh. Here in this room he had risen in cold dawns to the forlorn cry of starlings answering the toning of many bells; and through a window he saw the sunless dome of Saint Peter's that did not comfort.

In the late afternoon, a little before dusk, the skies cleared as he was walking through the Borghese Gardens; and suddenly before him, in a green clearing under great green trees, a flock of little girls from a convent were there playing and singing on the cold grass. Four white nuns watched over them. Here in the gardens in late pale sunlight there danced and whirled all these little girls. He went closer and lay on his stomach in the grass at the edge of the dancing green and watched them. Some who had fallen or rolled in the new grass had the stain of green on their pink dresses. Some wore earrings they had made out of grass buds, or bracelets and necklaces woven of grass and early poppies; and watching them as he lay in the grass, there cleared in his mind an old confusion of a faraway afternoon, in one Maytime.

It was a memory of a sunny May afternoon in Woodland Park in faraway Texas with a soft wind in the great pine trees under which the school had made a clearing for the Grammar School May Fete. This was an enchanted day, and the brother's costume as the king of flowers was ready and his sister's as a poppy was finally made. The brother had a silver wand, a silver crown made of nothing but cardboard but dazzled over with silver paper, and the crown and wand lay waiting beyond his touch on top of the glass china closet that had been his grandmother's. (The brother kept the crown for many years, though the stars soon fell off and the silver burnished quickly; and lying there in the grass he wished that he might have it again, though it would change nothing.)

The sister's dress was a poppy, all of crepe paper, crimson and green, and for her head there was a little cap of an inverted poppy bloom with the green stem on it. Her costume lay spread on the bed in the extra bedroom that was to become her own when she was old enough to take it and no longer afraid to sleep away from the rest of the family. It was the most fragile dress, sewn with such distress by the mother who every day had spoken of the difficulty of it and how she thought she would never make it right if she had all her life to try. It did not last nearly so long as the brother's king's crown and his silver wand.

May Day seemed never to arrive but always hung at the edge of Thursday, until suddenly it was there, and there was the little family walking on the way to Woodland Park, the children in their costumes finally their own, holding hands and leading the way, the mother and father marching behind. The mother's eyes watched with a look of resignation the imperfect stem drooping on the sister's head as she walked carefully ahead. The brother could not see his crown, but he knew the sunshine was making it glisten, for he could see the way the silver wand, which he held very carefully as he walked, shone in the golden May Day light. The sister walked never so carefully in her life so as not to spoil her poppy dress, because her mother had warned her severely that the crepe paper would stretch out of shape or perhaps even "shatter," it was so ephemeral as any bloom, if she leapt or ran. The brother wondered how she could possibly dance the Maypole dance in it. She would have to do it very delicately.

At Woodland Park, a wide green slope on the banks of the Chocolate Bayou, there was a resplendent May crowd standing and walking about. There were gay lemonade booths decorated with colored papers, kiosks with colored lanterns swinging in the breeze, tent-topped stands where ices were sold, rustling in layers of Dennison paper and flags of ribbons. In the middle of the park was the clearing and in the center of the clearing was the grand Maypole, tall and strong, with its blue and white paper streamers drawn down and held in place at its base, waiting for each dancer's hand to take its own. The wind was trilling the whole delicate construction and there was such a silken rustling sound of paper and leaves that the whole frail world seemed to be made of leaf and bloom, all trembling and shining in sunlight and wind. How one hoped that the Maypole dancers would do it right, as they had been instructed through so many days of practice in the school auditorium. They had only one chance. Everything had the feeling of extreme delicacy and momentariness on this transient afternoon, an expendable moment of May, that rain could fade and wilt, wind could tear and blow away.

The sister found her assembling group of friends who were flowers: roses, tulips, lilies, and a few difficult wisterias.

The mothers had done a good job of making the costumes, under the teachers' guidance. They had spent two tedious weeks all sewing delicate stuff in one of the classrooms after school.

As the brother was the king of flowers, he had to stand alone at his place of entrance, for there was no queen of flowers . . . why, one did not know or had not even thought of. The brother's costume was only a black suit, but his very first to own, coat and trousers, and a white shirt and tie; and that in itself was enough to make it a special day. But it was the crown and the wand that made all the difference. His task would be to move among the folded girls, all in a crowd, and gently touch each of them with his wand and so bring them up to bloom, while the lovely but somehow so deeply sad music of "Welcome, Sweet Springtime" played out from the piano. He waited with thrilling fright. He was second on the program, since the first thing was the entrance and procession of the King and Queen of May with all their court.

It began, and a boy walked out stiffly from the crowd, took his place by the empty throne and blew a fanfare as clear as sunshine on his bugle. He blew it right, thank goodness, and for the first time; and so there was no danger of giggles among the flowers who had not been able to control themselves during rehearsals when the bugle blurted and made no fanfare whatsoever. After the perfect fanfare, everyone was very quiet and the piano began. The court entered the clearing. The brother began to have a throbbing headache and to feel deeply sick. Out came the flower girls, the littlest, throwing rose petals to make a path for the king and queen; but the jester who followed, all in bells and pointed paper, kicked up the petals, against admonitions in rehearsals, and this was the first wrong thing. Yet how could he avoid tromping the blossoms? The brother grew sicker. Then the princesses came, teased, then the princes, the dukes and duchesses, and finally the king and queen, whom the school had voted for. The piano was rolling out its coronation march when the brother ran behind it, the music bursting in his head, and vomited there behind the piano, holding the crown with both hands to keep it from falling. He thought he might die from sickness and fright. But he felt better, now, though shamed, and he went back to his place. Now the court was seated, and without mishap, looking like a whole garden of flowers, and there was great applause. A pause, and then the familiar melody of "Welcome, Sweet Springtime," which had haunted him ever since they had begun practicing, filled the air. Suddenly all the flowers ran out into the clearing and fell to the ground around the Maypole, finding their streamers.

Then in a moment of blindness and exaltation, the brother heard his cue of music and it was time for him to come in among the flowers. He did not know what he did, but he remembered only a feeling of deep sadness and loveliness as he entered the clearing and moved among the folded flowers, touching each with his silver wand and bringing each up to flowering, all the beautiful little girls who so long ago vanished to many places and none ever so wild and shy again as that afternoon in a golden park of pine trees and flowers; and the whole Maypole began to open out like an enormous paper parasol. The brother knew when he came to the poppy that was his sister, for in an instant he saw, as he lowered his wand, that green fault in the stem which his mother had been so grieved at not being able to make properly, though the other mothers had said it would do and not to worry about it; and in the last weeks it had become the anxiety of the household. Once the mother even wept with despair over the stem and said, biting her lip and looking out the window, "I just cannot make it right"; and he had heard his mother and father speaking softly about it in the night. "It will be all right if you don't make it just perfect," the father had consoled her. "Children don't notice those little things." The brother and sister had been worried about the stem and wished, as they walked to school, that their mother could make it right. The brother even prayed for it at night, finishing his memorized prayer with "Lord help my mother make the poppy stem right." Then it was, at that instant, as he lowered his wand to touch it, that the little green stem seemed the fault in the household and a symbol of loving imperfection.

The brother touched with trembling wand the green stem on his sister's head, and he felt his sister shy at the glancing touch of it, saw her rise halfway as if in a spell and saw her trod a petal of her dress; and then he watched her stumble and fall, as if  he had struck her with a burning rod.

He saw, in a mist of tears, a vision of his mother and his father and his sister and himself standing together in the clearing on the throne of May that was emptied of its royalty and where they had been brought to dock, ruiners of May, and the Maypole a twisted stalk of knotted paper behind them, casting shadow over them, his sister in her withered poppy dress and he in his suit with his burnished crown fallen down over his eyes like a blindfold and holding the silver wand that mocked him, his mother aggrieved and his father humbled; and he heard the thunderous laughter and soughing sigh, like a storm in the trees, of a vast crowd of May persons who, dressed in paper and leaves and petals, seemed to have come for a moment out of the trees and the grass and the rushes of the bayou that ran below the clearing, an assembly of judges and mockers and revelers, demoniacal and green and accusing. How cruel and how lovely was May, when everything was impetuous and passionate and merciless. And he could hear his mother's voice before the green jury, "I just could not make it right," and his father's, "We never had a chance, any of us, my mother and my father and my brothers and my sisters"; and the brother could feel his own wordless answer stirring in his depths where it would not for so long to come rise and be uttered.

The brother reeled back from his sister for a moment, but for some reason which he could not understand until many years later, until this moment when he lay in the grass of a foreign city on the rim of a little park where a crowd of orphan children played on the grass, he could not move himself to help his sister up. She had torn her frail paper dress; she was crying. The brother stood over his sister and his wand hung from his limp hand and dragged the ground and he began to cry, too, and there was a long interruption with the sister and brother crying, flower and king of flowers in the green clearing in the sunshine circled round by a world of faces, friend and stranger, all people of May, the music of "Welcome, Sweet Springtime" playing on, so very sorrowful now, it seemed a dirge of winter. Some of the flowers not yet brought to bloom by the wand could not restrain themselves from peeping up to see what had happened, and the whole garden was on the verge of shattering. In another minute a teacher had rushed out to help the sister up and motioned to the brother to go on. Yet he had not been able to help his sister come to flower, as he or nothing in this world could help his mother make the proper stem; and in that moment he knew certainly that no one ever could mend certain flaws, no mother's hands or brother's wand but some hand of God or wand of wind or rain, something like that, beyond the touch of human hands.

When the whole garden of flowers was in full perfect bloom, except for the blight of his sister whose dress was torn and one petal dragging behind her, and the Maypole opened out and trembling in the sunlight, the brother backed away from the clearing and into the crowd and found his way to hide behind the piano where he wept bitterly as it went on playing the sad springtime air. His throat ached, scorched with the lime of grief for his sister, for his mother, for this bitter time of May, and for his first suit and tie which seemed, then, to have something to do with some deep disaster of afternoon that even the crown and the wand could not alter or transform.

Behind the piano he wept bitterly in honor of more than he could know then. And he felt again as he had so many times before, already, in his very beginning life, that gentle blue visitation of a sense of tragic unfulfillment, a doom of incompleteness in his heritage, never quite brought to perfect bloom, as though its lighted way had been crossed by a shadow of error; and mistouched, stumbling, bearing its flaw upon its brow and shying for the touch of a magical wand, it could not rise, but struggling to rise it tore its flesh and limped into its dance.

Now the flowers were standing in their circle round the unfurled Maypole and in another minute they were dancing the Maypole dance, and the sister was there. The brother saw his sister dancing round and round, weaving her blue ribbon in and out without one mistake, pale and innocent and melancholy in her torn dress, dragging along with her while she leapt, as if she were a little lame, the broken petal of the dress that seemed already to be withering, and upon her forehead the blighted stem drooped and bobbled, grotesque and mocking like a little green horn on her brow; and the brother saw, as the whole May Fete witnessed, that surely the sister was the serenest performer of all the Maypole dancers, an aerial creature wan from early failure, touched with some pale light, skipping and singing softly in a visionary moment of unearthly beauty; and he, like her, in those moments, felt touched, too, by that wand of delicate heartbreak held by the demon king that lives in May, that momentary month that would pass and never come again until the world and all its flowers and grass had been touched and brazed by the summer sun, burnt by the frosts of autumn and buried under winter . . . until the Maypole's ribbons of paper would fade and the poppy dress shatter, the wand tarnish and the cardboard crown moult its silver stars.

Then, there in the center of the green at the end of this hazardous performance, all the dancers gone away, stood the enduring Maypole woven and plaited without one mistake; and in the empty clearing there lay upon the mown grass of May the lost petal from the poppy dress.

Now he was watching and hearing the little girls in the Borghese Gardens, again; but after another moment he was standing, and then, looking back at them, he walked away, touching with the fingers that had long ago held the magic wand the stain of grass on his white trousers. Bitter grass! The bitter water of the fountains of this eternal city is surely for the watering of grass, he thought. Bitter love of God that suffers for this majestic perishability that the planting wind blows over and withers! Bitter May! Bitter flesh, bearing upon it the ineradicable stain that tells the story of this oh great glory of flesh of grass!

In his alien room of ancient floor, round which the denouncing cry of the demon starlings whirled, he pondered the passing of early revelations, how they sink through the currents of years, their adornment dissolving away like petals of paper and pasted stars; and, at long last, shelled of embellishment and ungarnished, settle on the cold hard utter bottom and foundation of unalterable truth.

*from The Uncollected Works*

# Figure Over The Town

I N the town of my beginning I saw this masked figure sitting aloft. It was never explained to me by my elders, who were thrilled and disturbed by the figure too, who it was, except that he was called Flagpole Moody. The days and nights he sat aloft were counted on calendars in the kitchens of small houses and in troubled minds, for Flagpole Moody fed the fancy of an isolated small town of practical folk whose day's work was hard and real.

Since the night he was pointed out to me from the roof of the little shed where my father sheltered grain and plowing and planting implements, his shape has never left me; in many critical experiences of my life it has suddenly appeared before me, so that I have come to see that it is a dominating emblem of my life, as often a lost lover is, or the figure of a parent, or the symbol of a faith, as the scallop shell was for so many at one time, or the Cross.

It was in the time of a war I could not understand, being so very young, that my father came to me at darkening, in the beginning wintertime, and said, "Come with me to the Patch, Son, for I want to show you something."

The Patch, which I often dream about, was a mysterious fenced-in plot of ground, about half an acre, where I never intruded. I often stood at the gate or fence and looked in through the hexagonal lenses of the chicken wire and saw how strange this little territory was, and wondered what it was for. There was the shed in it where implements and grain were stored, but nothing was ever planted nor any animal pastured here; nothing, not even grass or weed, grew here; it was just plain common ground.

This late afternoon my father took me into the Patch and led me to the shed and hoisted me up to the roof. He waited a moment while I looked around at all the world we lived in and had forgotten was so wide and housed so many in dwellings quite like ours. (Later, when my grandfather, my father's father, took me across the road and railroad tracks into a large pasture—so great I had thought it, from the window of our house, the whole world—where a little circus had been set up as if by magic the night before, and raised me to the broad back of a sleepy elephant, I saw the same sight and recalled not only the night I stood on the roof of the shed, but also what I had seen from there, that haunting image, and thought I saw it again, this time on the lightning rod of our house . . . but no, it was, as always, the crowing cock that stood there, eternally strutting out his breast and at the break of crowing.)

My father waited, and when he saw that I had steadied myself, he said, "Well, Son, what is it that you see over there, by the Methodist church?"

I was speechless and could only gaze; and then I finally said to him, not moving, "Something is sitting on the flagpole on top of a building."

"It is just a man," my father said, "and his name is Flagpole Moody. He is going to sit up there for as long as he can stand it."

When we came into the house, I heard my father say to my mother, lightly, "I showed Son Flagpole Moody and I think it scared him a little." And I heard my mother say, "It seems a foolish stunt, and I think maybe children shouldn't see it."

All that night Flagpole Moody was on my mind. When it began raining, in the very deepest night, I worried about him in the rain, and I went to my window and looked out to see if I could see him. When it lightninged, I saw that he was safe and dry under a little tent he had raised over himself. Later I had a terrible dream about him, that he was falling, falling, and when I called out in my nightmare, my parents came to me and patted me back to sleep, never knowing that I would dream of him again.

He stayed and stayed up there, the flagpole sitter, hooded (why would he not show his face?), and when we were in town and walked under him, I would not look up as they told me to; but once, when we stood across the street from the building where he was perched, I looked up and saw how high he was in the air, and he waved down at me with his cap in his hand.

Everywhere there was the talk of the war, but where it was or what it was I did not know. It seemed only some huge appetite that craved all our sugar and begged from the town its goods, so that people seemed paled and impoverished by it, and it made life gloomy—that was the word. One night we went into the town to watch them burn Old Man Gloom, a monstrous straw man with a sour, turned-down look on his face and dressed even to the point of having a hat—it was the Ku Klux Klan who lit him afire—and above, in the light of the flames, we saw Flagpole Moody waving his cap to us. He had been up eighteen days.

He kept staying up there. More and more the talk was about him, with the feeling of the war beneath all the talk.

People began to get restless about Flagpole Moody and to want him to come on down. "It seems morbid," I remember my mother saying. What at first had been a thrill and an excitement—the whole town was there every other day when the provisions basket was raised up to him, and the contributions were extravagant: fresh pies and cakes, milk, little presents, and so forth—became an everyday sight; then he seemed ignored and forgotten by the town except for me, who kept a constant, secret watch on him; then, finally, the town became disturbed by him, for he seemed to be going on and on; he seemed an intruder now. Who could feel unlooked at or unhovered over in his house with this figure over everything? (It was discovered the Flagpole was spying on the town through binoculars.) There was an agitation to bring him down and the city council met to this end.

There had been some irregularity in the town which had been laid to the general lawlessness and demoralizing effect of the war: robberies; the disappearance of a beautiful young girl, Sarah Nichols (but it was said she ran away to find someone in the war); and one Negro shot in the woods, which could have been the work of the Ku Klux Klan. The question at the city-council meeting was, "Who gave Flagpole Moody permission to go up there?" No one seemed to know; the merchants said it was not for advertising, or at least no one of them had arranged it, though after he was up, many of them tried to use him to advertise their products—Egg Lay or Red Goose Shoes or Have a Coke at Robbins Pharmacy—and why not? The Chamber of Commerce had not brought him, nor the Women's Club; maybe the Ku Klux had, to warn and tame the Negroes, who were especially in awe of Flagpole Moody; but the Klan was as innocent as all the others, it said. The pastor was reminded of the time a bird had built a nest on the church steeple, a huge foreign bird that had delighted all the congregation as well as given him subject matter for several sermons; he told how the congregation came out on the grounds to adore the bird, which in time became suddenly savage and swooped to pluck the feathers from women's Sunday hats and was finally brought down by the fire department, which found the nest full of rats and mice, half devoured, and no eggs at all—this last fact the subject of another series of sermons by the paster, drawing as he did his topics from real life.

As the flagpole sitter had come to be regarded as a defacement of the landscape, an unsightly object, a tramp, it was suggested that the Ku Klux Klan build a fire in the square and ride round it on their horses and in their sheets, firing their guns into the air, as they did in their public demonstrations against immorality, to force Flagpole down. If this failed, it was suggested someone should be sent up on a firemen's ladder to reason with Flagpole. He was regarded now as a *danger* to the town, and more, as a kind of criminal. (At first he had been admired and respected for his courage, and desired, even: many women had been intoxicated by him, sending up, in the provisions basket, love notes and photographs of themselves, which Flagpole had read and then sailed down for anyone to pick up and read, to the embarrassment of this woman and that. There had been a number of local exposures.)

The town was ready for any kind of miracle or sensation, obviously. A fanatical religious group took Flagpole Moody for the Second Coming. The old man called Old Man Nay, who lived on the edge of the town in a boarded-up house and sat at the one open window with his shotgun in his lap, watching for the Devil, unnailed his door and appeared in the square to announce that he had seen a light playing around Flagpole at night and that Flagpole was some phantom representative of the Devil and should be banished by a raising of the Cross; but others explained that what Old Man Nay saw was St. Elmo's fire, a natural phenomenon. Whatever was given a fantastical meaning by some was explained away by others as of natural cause. What was right? Who was to believe what?

An evangelist who called himself "The Christian Jew" had, at the beginning, requested of Flagpole Moody, by a letter in the basket, the dropping of leaflets. A sample was pinned to the letter. The leaflet, printed in red ink, said in huge letters across the top: WARNING! YOU ARE IN GREAT DANGER! Below was a long message to sinners. If Flagpole would drop these messages upon the town, he would be aiding in the salvation of the wicked. "The Judgments of God are soon to be poured upon the Earth! Prepare to meet God before it is too late! Where will you spend Eternity? What can you do to be saved? How shall we escape if we neglect so great salvation! (Heb. 2:3)."

But there was no reply from Flagpole, which was evidence enough for the Christian Jew to know that Flagpole was on the Devil's side. He held meetings at night in the square, with his little group of followers passing out the leaflets.

"Lower Cain!" he bellowed. "You sinners standing on the street corner running a long tongue about your neighbors; you show-going, card-playing, jazz-dancing brothers—God love your soul—you are a tribe of sinners and you know it and God knows it, but He loves you and wants you to come into His tabernacle and give up your hearts that are laden with wickedness. If you look in the Bible, if you will turn to the chapter of Isaiah, you will find there about the fallen angel, Lucifer was his name, and how his clothing was sewn of emeralds and sapphires, for he was very beautiful; but friends, my sinloving friends, that didn't make any difference. 'How art thou fallen from Heaven, O Lucifer, son of the morning!' the Bible reads. And it says there that the Devil will walk amongst us and that the Devil will sit on the rooftops; and I tell you we must unite together to drive Satan from the top of the world. Listen to me and read my message, for I was the rottenest man in this world until I heard the voice of God. I drank, I ran with women, I sought after the thrills of the flesh . . . and I admonish you that the past scenes of earth *shall be remembered in Hell.*"

The old maid, Miss Hazel Bright, who had had one lover long ago, a cowboy named Rolfe Sanderson who had gone away and never returned, told that Flagpole was Rolfe come back, and she wrote notes of poetic longing to put in the provisions basket. Everybody used Flagpole Moody for his own purpose, and so he, sitting away from it all, apparently serene in his own dream and idea of himself, became the lost lover to the lovelorn, the saint to the seekers of salvation, the scapegoat of the guilty, the damned to those who were lost.

The town went on tormenting him; they could not let him alone. They wished him to be their own dream or hope or lost illusion, or they wished him to be what destroyed hope and illusion. They wanted something they could get their hands on; they wanted someone to ease the dark misgiving in themselves, to take to their deepest bosom, into the farthest cave of themselves where they would take no other if he could come and be for them alone. They plagued him with love letters, and when he would not acknowledge these professions of love, they wrote him messages of hate.

They told him their secrets, and when he would not show himself to be overwhelmed, they accused him of keeping secrets of his own. They professed to be willing to follow him, leaving everything behind, but when he would not answer "come," they told him how they wished he would fall and knock his brains out. They could not make up their minds and they tried to destroy him because he had made up his, whatever it was he had made his mind up to.

Merchants tormented him with proposals and offers— would he wear a Stetson hat all one day, tip and wave it to the people below? Would he hold, just for fifteen minutes every hour, a streamer with words on it proclaiming the goodness of their bread, or allow balloons, spelling out the name of something that ought to be bought, to be floated from the flagpole? Would he throw down Life Savers? Many a man, and most, would have done it, would have supplied an understandable reason for his behavior, pacifying the general observer, and in the general observer's own terms (or the general observer would not have it), and so send him away undisturbed, with the feeling that all the world was really just as he was, cheating a little here, disguising a little there. (Everybody was, after all, alike, so where the pain, and why?)

But Flagpole Moody gave no answer. Apparently he had nothing to sell, wanted to make no fortune, to play no jokes or tricks; apparently he wanted just to be let alone to do his job. But because he was so different, they would not let him alone until they could, by whatever means, make him quiet like themselves, or cause him, at least, to recognize them and pay *them* some attention. Was he camping up there for the fun of it? If so, why would he not let them all share in it? Maybe he was there for the pure devilment of it, like a cat calm on a chimney top. Or for some very crazy and not-to-be-tolerated reason of his own (which everyone tried to make out, hating secrets as people do who want everything in the clear, where they can attack it and feel moral dudgeon against it).

Was it Cray McCreery up there? Had somebody made him another bet? One time Cray had walked barefooted to the next town, eighteen miles, because of a lost bet. But no, Cray McCreery was found, as usual, in the Domino Parlor. Had any crazy people escaped from the asylum? They were counted and found to be all in. The mind reader, Madame Fritzie, was importuned: There seemed, she said, to be a dark woman in the picture; that was all she contributed: "I see a dark woman . . ." And as she had admonished so many in the town with her recurring vision of a dark woman, there was either an army of dark women tormenting the minds of men and women in the world, or only one, which was Madame Fritzie herself. She could have made a fortune out of the whole affair if she had had her wits about her. More than one Ouija board was put questions to, but the answers were either indistinguishable or not to the point.

Dogs howled and bayed at night and sometimes in the afternoons; hens crowed; the sudden death of children was laid to the evil power of Flagpole Moody over the town.

A masked buffoon came to a party dressed as Flagpole Moody and caused increasing uneasiness among the guests until three of the men at the party, deciding to take subtle action rather than force the stranger to unmask, reported to the police by telephone. The police told them to unmask him by force and they were coming. When the police arrived they found the stranger was Marcus Peters, a past president of the Lions Club and a practical joker with the biggest belly laugh in town, and everybody would have known all along who the impostor was if he had only laughed.

A new language evolved in the town: "You're crazy as Moody," "cold as a flagpole sitter's——," "go sit on a flagpole" and other phrases of that sort.

In that day and time there flourished, even in that little town, a group of sensitive and intellectual people, poets and artists and whatnot, who thought themselves quite mad and gay—and quite lost, too, though they would turn their lostness to a good thing. These advanced people needed an object upon which to hinge their loose and floating cause, and they chose Flagpole Moody to draw attention, which they so craved, to themselves. They exalted him with some high, esoteric meaning that they alone understood, and they developed a whole style of poetry, music and painting, the echoes of which are still heard, around the symbol of Flagpole Moody. They wrote, and read aloud to meetings, critical explanations of the Theory of Aloftness.

Only Mrs. T. Trever Sanderson was bored with it all, shambling restlessly about the hospital in her Japanese kimono, her spotted hands (liver trouble, the doctors said) spread like fat lizards on the knolls of her hips. She was there again for one of her rest cures, because her oil-money worries were wearing her to death, and now the Catholic Church was pursuing her with zeal to convert her—for her money, so she said. Still, there was something to the Catholic Church; you couldn't get around that, she said, turning her spotted hands to show them yellow underneath, like a lizard's belly; and she gave a golden windowpane illustrating *The Temptation of St. Anthony* to St. Mary's Church, but would do no more than that.

There were many little felonies and even big offenses of undetermined origin in the police records of the town, and

Flagpole was a stimulus to the fresh inspection of unsolved crimes. He drew suspicions up to him and absorbed them like a filter, as though he might purify the town of wickedness. If only he would send down some response to what had gone up to him. But he would not budge; and now he no longer even waved to the people below as he had during the first good days. Flagpole Moody had utterly withdrawn from everybody. What the town finally decided was to put a searchlight on him at night, to keep watch on him.

With the searchlight on the flagpole sitter, the whole thing took a turn, became an excuse for a ribald attitude. When a little wartime carnival came to town, it was invited to install itself in the square, and a bazaar was added to it by the town. The spirit of Flagpole had to be admired, it was admitted; for after a day and night of shunning the gaiety and the mockery of it all, he showed his good nature and good sportsmanship—even his daring—by participating! He began to do what looked like acrobatic stunts, as though he were an attraction of the carnival.

And what did the people do, after a while, but turn against him again and say he was, as they had said at first, a sensationalist? Still, I loved it that he had become active; that it was not a static, fastidious, precious and Olympian show, that Flagpole did not take on a self-righteous or pompous or persecuted air, although my secret conception of him was still a tragic one. I was proud that my idea fought back—otherwise he was like Old Man Gloom, a shape of straw and sawdust in man's clothing, and let them burn him, if only gloom stood among the executioners, watching its own effigy and blowing on the flames. I know now that what I saw was the conflict of an idea with a society; and I am sure that the idea was bred by the society—raised up there, even, by the society—in short, society was in the flagpole sitter and he was in the society of the town.

There was, at the little carnival, one concession called "Ring Flagpole's Bell." It invited customers to try to strike a bell at the top of a tall pole resembling his—and with a replica of him on top—by hitting a little platform with a rubber-headed sledgehammer; this would drive a metal disk up toward the bell. There was another concession where people could throw darts at a target resembling a figure on a pole. The Ferris wheel was put so close to Flagpole that when its passengers reached the top they could almost, for a magical instant, reach over and touch his body. Going round and round, it was as if one were soaring up to him only to fall away, down, from him; to have him and to lose him; and it was all felt in a marvelous whirling sensation in the stomach that made this experience the most vaunted of the show.

This must have tantalized Flagpole, and perhaps it seemed to him that all the beautiful and desirable people in the world rose and fell around him, offering themselves to him only to withdraw untaken and ungiven, a flashing wheel of faces, eyes, lips and sometimes tongues stuck out at him and sometimes a thigh shown, offering sex, and then burning away. His sky at night was filled with voluptuous images, and often he must have imagined the faces of those he had once loved and possessed, turning round and round his head to torment him. But there were men on the wheel who made profane signs to him, and women who thumbed their noses.

Soon Flagpole raised his tent again and hid himself from his tormentors. What specifically caused his withdrawal was the attempt of a drunken young man to shoot him. This young man, named Maury, rode a motorcycle around the town at all hours and loved the meaner streets and the women who gave him ease, especially the fat ones, his mania. One night he stood at the hotel window and watched the figure on the pole, who seemed to flash on and off, real and then unreal, with the light of the electric sign beneath the window. He took deep drags off his cigarette and blew the smoke out toward Flagpole; then he blew smoke rings as if to lasso Flagpole with them, or as if his figure were a pin he could hoop with the rings of smoke. "You silly bastard, do you like what you see?" he had muttered, and "Where have I seen you before?" between his half-clenched teeth, and then he had fired the pistol. Flagpole turned away then, once and for all.

But he had not turned away from me. I, the silent observer, watching from my window or from any high place I could secretly climb to, witnessed all this conflict and the tumult of the town. One night in my dreaming of Flagpole Moody—it happened every night, this dream, and in the afternoons when I took my nap, and the dreaming had gone on so long that it seemed, finally, as if he and I were friends, that he came down secretly to a rendezvous with me in the little pasture, and it was only years later that I would know what all our conversations had been about—that night in my dream the people of the town came to me and said, "Son, we have chosen you to go up the flagpole to Flagpole Moody and tell him to come down."

In my dream they led me, with cheers and honors, to the top of the building and stood below while I shinnied up the pole. A great black bird was circling over Flagpole's tent. As I went up the pole I noticed crowded avenues of ants coming and going along the pole. And when I went into the tent, I found Flagpole gone. The tent was as if a tornado had swept through the whole inside of it. There were piles of rotten food; shreds of letters torn and retorn, as small as flakes of snow; photographs pinned to the walls of the tent were marked and scrawled over so that they looked like photographs of fiends and monsters; corpses and drifts of feathers of dead birds that had flown at night into the tent and gone so wild with fright that they had beaten themselves to death against the sides. And over it all was the vicious traffic of insects that had found the remains, in the way insects sense what human beings have left, and come from miles away.

What would I tell them below, those who were now crying up to me, "What does he say, what does Flagpole Moody say?" And there were whistles and an increasingly thunderous chant of "Bring him down! Bring him down! Bring him down!" What would I tell them? I was glad he had gone; but I would not tell them that—yet. In the tent I found one little thing that had not been touched or changed by Flagpole; a piece of paper with printed words, and across the top the huge red words: WARNING! YOU ARE IN GREAT DANGER!

Then, in my dream, I went to the flap of the tent and stuck out my head. There was a searchlight upon me through which fell a delicate curtain of light rain; and through the lighted curtain of rain that made the people seem far, far below, under shimmering and jeweled veils, I shouted down to the multitude, which was dead quiet now, "He is not here! Flagpole Moody is not here!"

There was no sound from the crowd, which had not, at first, heard what I said. They waited; then one voice bellowed up, "Tell him to come down!" And others joined this voice until, again, the crowd was roaring, "Tell him that we will not harm him; only tell him he has to come down!" Then I waved down at them to be quiet, in Flagpole Moody's gesture of salute, as he had waved down at people on the sidewalks and streets. Again they hushed to hear me. Again I said, this time in a voice that was not mine, but large and round and resounding, "Flagpole Moody is not here. His place is empty."

And then, in my magnificent dream, I closed the flap of the tent and settled down to make Flagpole Moody's place my own, to drive out the insects, to erase the marks on the photographs, and to piece together, with infinite and patient care, the fragments of the letters to see what they told. It would take me a very long time, this putting together again what had been torn into pieces, but I would have a very long time to give to it, and I was at the source of the mystery, removed and secure from the chaos of the world below that could not make up its mind and tried to keep me from making up my own.

My dream ended here, or was broken, by the hand of my mother shaking me to morning; and when I went to eat breakfast I heard them saying in the kitchen that Flagpole Moody had signaled early, at dawn, around six o'clock, that he wanted to come down; that he had come down in his own time, and that he had come down very, very tired, after forty days and nights, the length of the Flood. I did not tell my dream, for I had no power of telling then, but I knew that I had a story to one day shape around the marvel and mystery that ended in a dream and began in the world that was to be mine.